Le

Farmer George, Volume 1
Volume 1

Lewis Melville

Farmer George, Volume 1
Volume 1

1st Edition | ISBN: 978-3-75241-644-2

Place of Publication: Frankfurt am Main, Germany

Year of Publication: 2020

Outlook Verlag GmbH, Germany.

Reproduction of the original.

FARMER GEORGE

BY

LEWIS MELVILLE

IN TWO VOLUMES

VOL. I

INTRODUCTION

This work is an attempt to portray the character of George III and to present him alike in his private life and in his Court. It is, therefore, not essential to the scheme of this book to treat of the political history of the reign, but it is impossible entirely to ignore it, since the King was so frequently instrumental in moulding it.[1] Only those events in which he took a leading part have been introduced, and consequently these volumes contain no account of Irish and Indian affairs, in which, apart from the Catholic Emancipation and East India Bills, the King did not actively interest himself.

This difficulty was not met with by the author when writing a book on the life and times of George IV,[2] because that Prince had little to do with politics. It is true that he threw his influence into the scale of the Opposition as soon as, or even before, he came of age, but this was for strictly personal reasons. Fox and Sheridan were the intimates of the later years of his minority, and his association with them gave him the pleasure of angering his father: it was his protest against George III for refusing him the income to which he considered himself, as Prince of Wales, entitled. He had, however, no interest in politics, as such, either before or after he ascended the throne; and, indeed, as King, the only measure that interested him was the Bill for the emancipation of the Catholics, which he opposed because resistance to it had made his father and his brother Frederick popular.

With George III the case was very different. He came to the throne in his twenty-third year, with his mother's advice, "Be King, George," ringing in his ears, and, fully determined to carry out this instruction to the best of his ability, he was not content to reign without making strenuous efforts to rule. "Farmer George," the nickname that has clung to him ever since it was bestowed satirically in the early days of his reign, has come, except by those well versed in the history of the times, to be accepted as a tribute to his simple-mindedness and his homely mode of living. To these it will come as a shock to learn that "Farmer George" was a politician of duplicity so amazing that, were he other than a sovereign, it might well be written down as unscrupulousness. Loyalty, indeed, seems to have been foreign to his nature: he was a born schemer. When the Duke of Newcastle was in power, George plotted for the removal of Pitt, knowing that the resignation of the "Great Commoner" must eventually bring about the retirement of the Duke, and so leave Bute in possession of supreme authority. When within a year "The Favourite" was compelled to withdraw, George, unperturbed, appointed George Grenville Prime Minister, but finding him unsubservient, intrigued against him, was found out, compelled to promise to abstain from further interference against his own ministers, broke his word again and again, and finally brought about the downfall of Grenville, who was succeeded by the Marquis of Rockingham. Again George employed the most unworthy means to get rid of Rockingham, and during the debates on the repeal of the Stamp Act encouraged his Household to vote against the Government, assuring them they should not lose their places, indeed would rise higher in his favour, because of their treachery to the head of the Administration of the Crown; and all the while he was writing encouraging notes to Rockingham assuring him of his support! This strange record of underhand intrigues has been traced in the following pages.

George had not even the excuse of success for his treachery. It is true that he contrived to compel the resignation of various ministers, but his incursions into the political arena were fraught with disaster. He forced Bute on the nation, and Bute could not venture to enter the City except with a band of prize-fighters around his carriage to protect him! He took an active part against Wilkes, and Wilkes became a popular hero! He encouraged the imposition of the Stamp Act in America, and in the end America was lost to England! Having no knowledge of men and being ignorant of the world, he was guided at first by secret advisers, and subsequently by his own likes and dislikes, coupled with a regard for his dignity, that did not, however, prevent him from personally canvassing Windsor in favour of the Court candidate when Keppel was standing for the parliamentary representation of the town.

George III was, according to his lights, a good man—

"I grant his household abstinence; I grant
His neutral virtues, which most monarchs want;"

a kind master; a well-meaning, though unwise father; a faithful husband, possessing

"that household virtue, most uncommon,
Of constancy to a bad, ugly woman,"

which was the more creditable as his nature was vastly susceptible. He was pious, anxious to do his duty, and deeply attached to his country, but believing himself always in the right, was frequently led by his feelings into courses such as justified Byron's magnificent onslaught:—

"In the first year of Freedom's second dawn
Died George the Third; although no tyrant, one
Who shielded tyrants, till each sense withdrawn
Left him nor mental nor external sun;
A better farmer ne'er brushed dew from lawn,
A worse king never left a realm undone.
He died—but left his subjects still behind,
One half as mad, and t'other no less blind."[3]

Yet, notwithstanding all the mistakes George III made, and all the mischief he did, his reign ended in a blaze of glory. England had survived the French Revolution without disastrous effects; and had taken a leading part in the subjugation of Napoleon. Nelson and Wellington, Wordsworth and Keats, Fox and Pitt, reflected their glory and the splendour of their actions upon the country of their birth. Yet—such is the irony of fate at its bitterest—while the world acknowledged the supremacy of England on land, at sea, and in commerce, while a whole people, delighted with magnificent achievements, acclaimed their ruler, crying lustily "God save the King," George, in whose name these great deeds were done, was but "a crazy old blind man in Windsor Tower."

"Give me a royal niche—it is my due,
The virtuousest king the realm ever knew.

I, through a decent reputable life,
Was constant to plain food and a plain wife.

Ireland I risked, and lost America;
But dined on legs of mutton every day.

My brain, perhaps, might be a feeble part;
But yet I think I had an English heart.

When all the Kings were prostrate, I alone
Stood face to face against Napoleon;

Nor ever could the ruthless Frenchman forge
A fetter for old England and old George.

I let loose flaming Nelson on his fleets;
I met his troops with Wellesley's bayonets.

Triumphant waved my flag on land and sea:
Where was the King in Europe like to me?

Monarchs exiled found shelter on my shores;
My bounty rescued Kings and Emperors.

[Pg xv]

But what boots victory by land and sea,
What boots that Kings found refuge at my knee?

I was a conqueror, but yet not proud;
And careless, even when Napoleon bow'd.

The rescued Kings came kiss my garments' hem:
The rescued Kings I never heeded them.

My guns roared triumph, but I never heard:
All England thrilled with joy, I never stirred.

What care had I of pomp, of fame, or power—
A crazy old blind man in Windsor Tower?"[4]

CHAPTER I

FREDERICK, PRINCE OF WALES

Historians have found something to praise in George I, and the bravery of George II on the field of battle has prejudiced many in favour of that monarch. George III has been extolled for his domestic virtues, and his successor held up to admiration for his courtly manners, while William IV found favour in the eyes of many for his homely air. Of all the Hanoverian princes in the direct line of succession to the English throne, alone Frederick Louis, Prince of Wales, lacks a solitary admirer among modern writers.

Frederick was born at Hanover on January 6, 1707, was there educated; and there, after the accession of George II to the English throne, remained, a mere lad, away from parental control, compelled to hold a daily Drawing-room, at which he received the adulation of unscrupulous and self-seeking courtiers in a dull, vulgar, and immoral Court. George II, remembering his behaviour to his father, was in no hurry to summon his son to England; and Frederick might have remained the ornament of the Hanoverian capital until his death, but that the English thought it advisable their future king should not be allowed to grow up in ignorance of the manners and customs of the land over which in the ordinary course of nature he would reign. Neither the King nor the Queen had any affection for the young man; and they were so reluctant to bring him into prominence, or even into frequent intercourse with themselves, that they disregarded the murmur of the people, and were inclined even to ignore the advice of the Privy Council—when news from Hanover caused them hurriedly to send for him.

Queen Sophia Dorothea of Prussia had years earlier said to Princess Caroline, afterwards Queen of England, "You, Caroline, Cousin dear, have a little Prince, Fritz, or let us call him *Fred*, since he is to be English; little Fred, who will one day, if all go right, be King of England. He is two years older than my little Wilhelmina, why should they not wed, and the two chief Protestant Houses, and Nations, thereby be united?" There was nothing to be said against this proposal, and much in its favour. "Princess Caroline was very willing; so was Electress Sophie, the Great-Grandmother of both the parties; so were the Georges, Father and Grandfather of Fred: little Fred himself was highly charmed, when told, of it; even little Wilhelmina, with her dolls, looked pleasantly demure on the occasion. So it remained settled in fact, though not in form; and little Fred (a florid milk-faced foolish kind of Boy, I guess), made presents to his little Prussian Cousin, wrote bits of love-letters to her and all along afterwards fancied himself, and at length ardently enough became, her little lover and intended—always rather a little fellow:—to which sentiments Wilhelmina signifies that she responded with the due maidenly indifference, but not in an offensive manner."[5] Then Prussian Fritz or Fred was born, and it was further agreed that Amelia, George II's second daughter, should marry him. George I sanctioned the arrangement, but the treaty in which it was incorporated was never signed; and on his accession, George II, for many reasons, was no longer desirous to carry out the marriage. Only Queen Sophia held to her project, and Frederick, the intended husband. The latter, doubtless incited by his father's opposition to imagine himself in love with Wilhelmina, caused it to be intimated to Queen Sophia that, if she would consent, he would travel secretly to Prussia and marry his cousin. The Queen was delighted, and summoned her husband to be present at the nuptials, but, anxious to share her joy, must needs select as a confidant the English ambassador Dubourgay, who, of course, could not treat such a communication as a confidence, and, to the Queen's horror, told her he must dispatch the news to his sovereign. In vain Sophia Dorothea pleaded for silence: it would spell ruin for it to be said that the envoy had known of the secret and had not informed his master. The only chance for the successful issue of the scheme was that Frederick should arrive before his father could interfere, but this was not to be. Colonel Launay came from England charged to return with the heir-apparent; and so the marriage was, at least, postponed. Frederick arrived in England on December 4, 1728, and early in the following year Sir Charles Hotham went as minister plenipotentiary to the King of Prussia to propose the carrying out of the double-marriage project, but while the latter was willing to consent to the marriage of his daughter with the Prince, he would not accept for his son the hand of Princess Amelia, declaring that he ought to espouse the Princess Royal. Neither party would give way, and the dislike of the potentates for each other resulted in 1730 in a definite rupture of the negotiations.

Photo by Emery Walker *From a painting by B. Dandridge*
FREDERICK, PRINCE OF WALES

On his arrival in England Frederick[6] was received with acclamation by the populace, but his relations with his parents were strained from the start. The original cause of quarrel is unknown to the present generation, and even at the time few were acquainted with it, though Sir Robert Walpole knew it, and Lord Hervey,[7] who wrote it down, only for his memorandum to be destroyed by his son, the Earl of Bristol.[8] It may be assumed, however, that his father's conduct in the negotiations for the marriage with the Princess of Prussia widened the breach. The Prince of Wales was certainly not an agreeable person. In Hanover he had indulged to excess in *"Wein, Weib, und Gesang,"* and he was the unfortunate possessor of a mean, paltry, despicable nature that revolted those with whom he was brought into contact. His mother hated him —"He is such an ass that one cannot tell what he thinks"; his sister Amelia loathed him and wished he were dead—"He is the greatest liar that ever spoke, and will put one arm round anybody's neck to kiss them, and then stab them with the other if he can"; and his father detested him. "My dear first born is the greatest ass, the greatest liar, the greatest *canaille* and the greatest beast in the whole world, and I heartily wish he was out of it," so said George II, and it must be conceded that in the main he was right.

Of course, the faults were not all on the side of the Prince of Wales: indeed, they were fairly evenly distributed between father and son. From the first he was publicly ignored by George II. "Whenever the Prince was in the room with the King it put one in mind of stories that one has heard of ghosts that appear to part of the company, and were invisible to the rest; and in this manner wherever the Prince stood, though the King passed him ever so often, or ever so near, it always seems as if the King thought the Prince filled a void of space."[9] The father took advantage of his position to keep the son short of money; and the son, after the manner of Hanoverian heirs-apparent, retorted by throwing himself into the arms of the Opposition. The Prince of Wales's great grievance was that he received an allowance only of £50,000 and that *at the King's pleasure*: and he contended that as George II, when Prince of Wales, had received £100,000 a year from George I's Civil List of £700,000, it was manifestly unfair that as the Civil List had been increased to £800,000, the Prince of Wales's income should be reduced by half and that dependent on the sovereign's humour.

Frederick, who had left Hanover in debt, had been further embarrassed in London, and, to free himself from financial trouble discussed with Sarah, Duchess of Marlborough, a marriage between himself and her granddaughter, Lady Diana Spencer,[10] conditional on the dowry being £100,000. The ambitious old lady was favourable to the scheme—it has been said, and perhaps with truth, that it was her proposal—and arrangements were made for the ceremony to take place privately at the Lodge in Windsor Great Park; but Sir Robert Walpole heard of it—that wily statesman learnt most secrets—and told the King, who forbade the marriage.

The Prince did not at first commit any serious offence against the King, but he contrived, with or without intention, to irritate or affront him almost daily. He wrote, or inspired, the "History of Prince Titi," in which the King and Queen were caricatured; and, with the guidance of Bubb Dodington,[11] formed a Court that became a *rendezvous* of the Opposition and the disaffected generally. It became his object in life to outshine his father in popularity, and as George II was not a favourite, and as Frederick could be agreeable when he wanted to make a good impression, and, besides, had the invaluable asset of a reasonable grievance, he did to a large extent succeed in his quest. "The Prince's character at his first coming over, though little more respectable, seemed much more amiable than, upon his opening himself further and being better known, it turned out to be; for, though there appeared nothing in him to be admired, yet there seemed nothing in him to be hated—neither anything great nor anything vicious. His behaviour was something that gained one's good wishes while it gave one no esteem for him, for his best qualities, whilst they prepossessed one the most in his favour, always gave one a degree of contempt for him at the same time."[12]

If George II was jealous of the Prince of Wales, the latter in turn was jealous of his sister, the Princess Royal, and he regarded it as a personal affront when in 1734 she was united to the Prince of Orange; thus, in spite of his two endeavours, marrying before him, and securing a settled income. A quarrel ensued, and the rivalry between the two convulsed the operatic world into which, being in itself *opera bouffe*, it was suitably carried. The Princess Royal was a friend and patron of Handel at the Haymarket Theatre: and therefore must her brother and his companions support the rival Buononcini at Lincoln's Inn Fields. The King and Queen sided with their daughter, and, says Hervey, "The affair grew as serious as that of the Greens and Blues under Justinian at Constantinople; and an anti-Handelist was looked upon as an anti-courtier, and voting against the Court in Parliament was hardly a less remissible or more venial sin than speaking against Handel or going to the Lincoln's Inn Fields Opera."[13] The victory in this Tweedledum-Tweedledee controversy fell to the Prince, though the sovereigns would not for a long time admit defeat, which gave Chesterfield[14] the opening for a *môt*: he told the Prince he had been that evening to the Haymarket Theatre, "but there being no one there but the King and Queen, and as I thought they might be talking business, I came away."

When the Princess Royal was married, the Prince of Wales presented himself before the King, and made three demands—permission to serve in the Rhine campaign, a settled and increased income, and a suitable marriage. George II gave an immediate and decided refusal to the first, but consented to consider the other proposals. As a result of negotiations arising from this conversation, the Prince of Wales married on April 26, 1736, Augusta, daughter of Frederick, Duke of Saxe-Gotha. There were great national rejoicings, and "I believe," said Horace Walpole, "the Princess will have more beauties bestowed on her by all the occasional poets than ever a painter would afford her. They will cook up a new Pandora, and in the bottom of the box enclose Hope that all they have said is true." Indeed, a salvo of eulogistic addresses in rhyme greeted the nuptial pair, headed by William Whitehead, the Laureate, who, on such occasions, could always be relied upon to write ridiculously fulsome lines.

> "Such was the age, so calm the earth's repose,
> When Maro sung, and a new Pollio rose.
> Oh! from such omens may again succeed
> Some glorious youth to grace the nuptial bed;
> Some future Scipio, good as well as great;
> Some young Marcellus with a better fate;
> Some infant Frederick, or some George to grace
> The rising records of the Brunswick race."

THE PRINCE AND PRINCESS OF WALES AND (IN THE BACKGROUND) MISS VANE AND HER SON

April 25th, 1736

The new Princess of Wales was a mere girl, straight from her mother's country house, and ignorant of courts, but not lacking self-possession nor good sense. "The Princess is neither handsome nor ugly, tall nor short, but has a lively, pretty countenance enough,"[15] and she found favour in the eyes of her husband, who, though attracted by her, was not content to be faithful. "The chief passion of the Prince was women," says Horace Walpole; "but, like the rest of his race, beauty was not a necessary ingredient." Soon after he came to England he had an intrigue with Anne Vane, the eldest daughter of Gilbert, Baron Barnard, and one of the Queen's maids of honour. "Beautiful Vanelia" was not immaculate, and she gave birth to a child in her apartments in St. James's Palace; the first Lord Hartington and Lord Hervey both believed themselves to be the father, but she, to make the most of her opportunity, wisely accredited the paternity to the Prince of Wales, who thus earned the undying hatred of Hervey.[16] The proud father then turned his attention to Lady Archibald Hamilton (wife of the Duke of Hamilton's brother), who had ten children, was neither young nor beautiful, but clever enough to let her husband believe she was faithful, although the intimacy between her and her royal lover was patent to all the world besides.

Realising the advisability to be off with the old love before he was on with the new, Frederick sent Lord Baltimore to Miss Vane, commanding her to live abroad for a period, on pain of forfeiting the allowance of £1,600 that he had made her since her dismissal from court—"if she would not live abroad, she might starve for him in England." Miss Vane sent for Hervey, who recommended her to refuse obedience—a step that infuriated the Prince with the adviser; but eventually she reminded her erstwhile lover of all she had sacrificed for the love she bore him, and this so tickled his vanity that not only did he permit her to retain her son and the income, and to remain in England, but gave her a house in Grosvenor Street wherein to live.

Following the example of George II, who had appointed his mistress, Mrs. Howard, to be woman of the bedchamber to his wife, Frederick made Lady Archibald Hamilton a lady-in-waiting to the Princess of Wales. Lady Archibald, however, was soon replaced in his favour by Lady Middlesex, who, although not good-looking, was the possessor of many accomplishments; but she had to be content to share his affections with Miss Granville and various opera dancers and singers.

The Prince, being unable to secure an increased income from his father, resorted to the usual princely device of borrowing money wherever he could get it. "They have found a way in the city to borrow £30,000 for the Prince at ten per cent. interest, to pay his crying debts to tradespeople; but I doubt that sum will not go very far," wrote the Duchess of Marlborough. "The salaries in the Prince's family are £25,000 a year, besides a good deal of expense at Cliefden in building and furniture; and the Prince and Princess's allowance for their clothes is £6,000 a year each. I am sorry there is such an increase in expense more than in former times, when there was more money a great deal: and I really think it would have been more for the Prince's interest if his counsellors had advised him to live only as a great man, and to give the reasons for it; and in doing so he would have made a better figure, and been safer, for nobody that does not get by it themselves can possibly think the contrary method a right one." The debts accumulated so rapidly, that there was really some show of reason for Lord Hervey (always on the look-out to revenge himself for the defection of his mistress) saying to the Queen that there actually "was danger of the King's days being shortened by the profligate usurers who lent the Prince of Wales money on condition of being paid at his Majesty's death, and who, he thought, would want nothing but a fair opportunity to hasten the day of payment; and the King's manner of exposing himself would make it easy for the usurers to accomplish such a design."[17]

Hitherto in his quarrels with his parents Frederick had not always been in the wrong, but in 1737 he committed an unpardonable offence in connexion with the birth of his first legitimate child, Augusta, afterwards Duchess of Brunswick, and the mother of Caroline, the unhappy consort of George IV. Though he had known for many months that the Princess of Wales was with child he did not inform his parents of the approaching event until July 5. But that was the least part of his transgression. Twice in that month he took the Princess secretly from Hampton Court to St. James's Palace, and on the second occasion, with only Lady Archibald Campbell in attendance, arrived in London but a few hours before the *accouchement*.

Photo by Emery Walker
From a portrait by Enoch Seaman
CAROLINE, CONSORT OF GEORGE II

Photo by Emery Walker
From a portrait by T. Worlidge
GEORGE II

The Queen had determined to be present at the birth.—"She [the Princess of Wales] cannot be brought to bed as quick as one can blow one's nose," she had told the King, "and I will be sure it is her child." Both were furious at being circumvented, and the King expressed his anger in no measured terms. "See now, with all your wisdom, how they have outwitted you," the King addressed his wife. "This is all your fault. There is a false child will be put upon you, and how will you answer it to all your children? This has been fine care and fine management for your son William: he is much indebted to you." The Queen drove to St. James's without delay, saw the child, and abandoned her suspicions. "God bless you, poor little creature," she said as she kissed it, "you have come into a disagreeable world." Had it been a big, healthy boy, instead of a girl, she said, she might not so readily have accepted the paternity claimed for it.

"The King has commanded me," Lord Essex[18] wrote from Hampton Court to the Prince of Wales on August 3, "to acquaint your Royal Highness that his Majesty most heartily rejoices at the safe delivery of the Princess; but that your carrying away of her Royal Highness from Hampton Court, the then residence of the King, the Queen, and the Royal Family, under the pains and certain indication of immediate labour, to the imminent danger and hazard both of the Princess and her child, and after sufficient warnings for a week before, to have made the necessary preparations for this happy event, without acquainting his Majesty, or the Queen, with the circumstances the Princess was in, or giving them the least notice of your departure, is looked upon by the King to be such a deliberate indignity offered to himself and to the Queen, that he resents it to the highest degree."[19]

A lengthy correspondence ensued, wherein, on the one hand, the Prince excused himself on the ground that the Princess was seized with the pains of labour earlier than was expected, and that at Hampton Court he was without a midwife or any assistance; and, on the other, the King declined to accept these reasons as true, refused to receive his son, and ordered him to leave St. James's as soon as possible, summing up the situation in a final letter, dated September 10.

"GEORGE R.

"The professions you have lately made in your letters, of your peculiar regards to me, are so contradictory to all your actions, that I cannot suffer myself to be imposed upon by them. You know very well you did not give the least intimation to me or to the Queen that the Princess was with child or breeding, until within less than a month of the birth of the young Princess: you removed the Princess twice in the week immediately preceding the day of her delivery from the place of my residence, in expectation, as you have voluntarily declared, of her labour; and both times upon your return, you industriously concealed from the knowledge of me and the Queen every circumstance relating to this important affair: and you, at last, without giving any notice to me, or to the Queen, precipitately hurried the Princess from Hampton Court, in a condition not to be named. After having thus, in execution of your own determined measures, exposed both the Princess and her child to the greatest perils, you now plead surprise and tenderness for the Princess, as the only motives that occasioned these repeated indignities offered to me and to the Queen your mother.

"This extravagant and undutiful behaviour in so essential a point as the birth of an heir to my crown, is such evidence to your premeditated defiance of me, and such a contempt of my authority and of the natural right belonging to your parents, as cannot be excused by the pretended innocence of your intentions, nor palliated or disguised by specious words only.

"But the whole tenour of your conduct for a considerable time has been so entirely void of all real duty to me, that I have long had reason to be highly offended with you. And until you withdraw your regard and confidence from those by whose instigation and advice you are directed and encouraged in your unwarrantable behaviour to me and your Queen, and until your return to your duty, you shall not reside in my palace: which I will not suffer to be made the resort of them who, under the appearance of an attachment to you, foment the division which you have made in my family, and thereby weaken the common interest of the whole.

"In the meantime, it is my pleasure that you leave St. James's with all your family, when it can be done without prejudice or inconvenience to the Princess. I shall for the present leave to the Princess the care of my granddaughter, until a proper time calls upon me to consider of her education.

"(signed) G. R." [20]

The Prince, through Lord Baltimore, expressed a desire to make a personal explanation to the Queen, who, through Lord Grantham, declined to receive it; and later the Princess, doubtless prompted by her husband, wrote to the King and Queen to express a desire for reconciliation, but in vain, for, in the sovereign's eyes, their son's offence was rank. Indeed, the King went so far as to print the correspondence between himself and the Prince of Wales, to which the latter made the effectual reply of publishing the not dissimilar letters of his father, when Prince of Wales, to George I. This reduced the King to impotent fury: he declared he did not believe Frederick could be his son, and insisted that he must be "what in German we call a *Wechselbalch*—I do not know if you have a word for it in English—it is not what you call a foundling, but a child put in a cradle instead of another."

What induced Frederick to risk the life of his wife and his unborn child, and to put to hazard the succession was a mystery at the time, and must for ever remain without satisfactory explanation. That it was done solely to annoy his parents seems insufficient reason, though it is all that offers, and Hervey suggests the hasty nocturnal removal was effected to prevent the presence of the Queen at the birth. This certainly seems insufficient to account for the unwarrantable proceeding, but no other solution offers itself.

The Prince of Wales had in 1730 taken a lease from the Capel family of Kew House (the fee of which was many years after purchased by George III from the Dowager Countess of Essex), and there he and his wife repaired for a while after being evicted from St. James's Palace; but soon they came back to London, and held their court, first at Norfolk House, St. James's Square, placed at their disposal by the Duke of Norfolk, and later at Leicester House, Leicester Square. The King expressed a wish that no one should visit his son, and actually caused it to be intimated to foreign ambassadors that to call on the Prince of Wales was objectionable to him; but this injunction was so generally disregarded that he took the extraordinary step of issuing, through his Chamberlain, a threat.

> "His Majesty, having been informed that due regard has not been paid to his order of September 11, 1737, has thought fit to declare that no person whatsoever, who shall go to pay their court to their Royal Highnesses, the Prince and Princess of Wales, shall be admitted into his Majesty's presence, at any of his royal palaces.
>
> "(signed) Grafton."

Even this measure failed of its effect, for while those who sought the King's favour had not been to Leicester House, the Opposition, knowing they had nothing to lose, were not affected by this command. Indeed, the Opposition, delighted to have so influential a chief, flocked around Frederick; and Bolingbroke,[21] Chesterfield, Pulteney,[22] Dodington, Carteret,[23] Wyndham,[24] Townshend[25] and Cobham,[26] were soon numbered among his regular visitors; while Huish has compiled a long list of peers[27] who frequently attended his *levées*.

The Prince made a very determined bid for popularity among all classes.

He put himself at the head of "The Patriots," and in 1739 recorded his first vote as a peer of Parliament against the Address and in favour of the war policy; subsequently, when war was declared, taking part with the Opposition in the public celebrations. He encouraged British manufactures, and neither he nor the Princess wore, or encouraged the wearing of, foreign materials. He gave entertainments to the nobility at his seat at Cliefden in Buckinghamshire, and visiting Bath in 1738, cleared the prison of all debtors and made a present of £1,000 towards the general hospital. Nor did he neglect letters and art, for which he had some slight regard. He patronised Thomson and Vertue the engraver, employed Dr. Freeman to write a "History of the English Tongue" as a text-book for Prince George and the younger princes;[28] sent two of his court to Cave, the publisher, to inquire the name of the author of the first issue of "The Rambler"; and exchanged badinage with Pope, whom he visited at Twickenham. Pope received him with great courtesy and expressions of attachment. "'Tis well," said Frederick, "but how shall we reconcile your love to a prince with your professed indisposition to kings, since princes will be kings in time?" "Sir," said the poet, "I consider Royalty under that noble and authorized type of the lion: while he is young and before his nails are grown, he may be approached and caressed with safety and pleasure."[29]

Frederick became very popular. "The truth is," Mr. McCarthy has said unkindly but with undoubted truth, "that the people in general, knowing little about the Prince, and knowing a great deal about the King, naturally leaned to the side of the man who might at least turn out to be better than his father."[30]

There was a general impression that he had been ill-treated, and there was a disposition among the lower classes to make amends for such a slight as having to live as a private gentleman at Norfolk House, without even the usual appanage of a sentry.

> "Some I have heard who speak this with rebuke,
> Guards should attend as well the prince as duke.
> Guards should protect from insult Britain's heir,
> Who greatly merits all the nation's care.
> Pleas'd with the honest zeal, they thus express,
> I tell them what each statesman must confess;
> No guard so strong, so noble, e'er can prove,
> As that which Frederick has—*a people's love.*"

"My God, popularity makes me sick; but Fritz's popularity makes me vomit," exclaimed the Queen, perhaps after hearing that when Frederick assisted to extinguish a fire, the mob cried, "Crown him! crown him!" "I hear that yesterday, on his side of the House, they talked of the King's being cast aside with the same *sang froid* as one would talk of a coach being overturned; and that my good son strutted about as if he had been already King. Did you mind the air with which he came into my Drawing-room in the morning, though he does not think fit to honour me with his presence or *ennui* me with that of his wife's of a night. I swear his behaviour shocked me so prodigiously that I could hardly bring myself to speak to him when he was with me afterwards; I felt something here in my throat that swelled and half choked me." The King was as bitter, and refused to admit Frederick to the Queen's deathbed. "His poor mother is not in a condition to see him act his false, whining, cringing tricks now," while the Queen declared that she was sure he wanted to see her only to have the delight of knowing she was dead a little sooner than if he had to await the tidings at home.

An attempt in 1742 to bring to an end the crying scandal of the open enmity between the King and the heir-apparent was made by Walpole, who thought, by detaching the Prince from the Opposition, to strengthen his steadily decreasing majority. The Bishop of Oxford[31] was sent to Norfolk House to intimate that if the Prince would make his peace with his father through the medium of a submissive letter, ministers would prevail upon the King to increase his income by £50,000, pay his debts to the tune of £200,000 and find places for his friends. The terms were tempting, but the Prince, knowing that Walpole's position was precarious, declined them, stating that he knew the offer came, not from the King, but from the minister, and that, while he would gladly be reconciled to his father, he could do so without setting a price upon it. "Walpole," he declared, "was a bar between the King and his people, between the King and foreign powers; between the King and himself." The refusal was politic, for Walpole was most unpopular. "I have *added* to the debt of the nation," so ran the inscription on a scroll issuing from the mouth of an effigy of Walpole, sitting between the King and the Prince; "I have *subtracted* from its glory; I have *multiplied* its embarrassments; and I have *divided* its Royal Family." The Prince's refusal to entertain the overture was a blow to the minister, who contended against a majority in the House of

Commons, until February 2, 1742, when he declared he would regard the question of the Chippenham election as a vote of confidence, and, if defeated upon it, would never again enter that House. He was beaten by sixteen, and on the 18th inst. took his seat "in another place" as the Earl of Oxford.

Immediately after Walpole's downfall, messages were exchanged between Norfolk House and St. James's, and on February 17 father and son met and embraced at the palace. The Prince's friends came into office, and so happy was the Prince that he testified to his joy by liberating four-and-twenty prisoners from his father's Bench—the amount of their debts being added to his own. He was indeed so overcome with delight at his virtue in being reconciled to his father that he ventured upon a joke when Mr. Vane, who was notoriously in the court interest, congratulated him on his reappearance at St. James's. "A vane," quoth he to the courtier, "is a weathercock, which turns with every gust of the wind, and therefore I dislike a vane." Witty, generous Prince!

The reconciliation was shortlived, and thereafter, for the rest of his life, Frederick was again in opposition to the court; but of these later years there is little or nothing to record, save that he solicited in vain the command of the royal army in the rebellion of '45. In March, 1751, he caught cold, and on the 20th inst., while, by his bedside, Desnoyers was playing the violin to amuse him, crying, "*Je sens la mort*," he expired suddenly—it is said from the bursting of an abscess which had been formed by a blow from a tennis ball. The King received the news at the whist table, and, showing neither surprise nor emotion, he crossed the room to where the Countess of Yarmouth sat at another table, and, after saying simply, "*Il est mort*," retired to his apartments. "I lost my eldest son," he remarked subsequently, "but I am glad of it."

The writers of the day were fulsome in their praise of the deceased Prince. Robert Southy says, Frederick died "to the unspeakable affliction of his royal consort, and the unfeigned sorrow of all who knew him;" and he sums him up as "a tender and obliging husband, a fond parent, a kind master, liberal, candid and humane, a munificent patron of the arts, an unwearied friend to merit, well-disposed to assert the rights of mankind, in general, and warmly attached to the interests of Great Britain."[32] In fact, Sir Galahad and the Admirable Crichton in one! Southy was not alone in his outspoken admiration, for Mr. McCarthy reminds us of a volume issued by Oxford University, "*Epicedia Oxoniensia in obitum celsissimi et desideratissimi Frederici Principis Walliæ*. Here all the learned languages, and not the learned languages alone, contributed the syllables of simulated despair. Many scholastic gentlemen mourned in Greek; James Stillingfleet found vent in Hebrew; Mr. Betts concealed his tears under the cloak of the Syriac speech;

George Costard sorrowed in Arabic that might have amazed Abu l'Atahiyeh; Mr. Swinton's learned sock stirred him to Phoenician and Etruscan; and Mr. Evans, full of national fire and the traditions of the bards, delivered himself, and at great length, too, in Welsh."[33] Amusing, too, was a sermon preached at Mayfair Chapel, in the course of which the preacher, lamenting the demise of the royal personage, declared that his Royal Highness "had no great parts, but he had great virtues; indeed, they degenerated into vices; he was very generous, but I hear his generosity has ruined a great many people; and then his condescension was such that he kept very bad company."

Very differently spoke those who knew the Prince. "He was indeed as false as his capacity would allow him to be, and was more capable in that walk than in any other, never having the least hesitation, from principle or fear of future detection, in telling any lie that served his future purpose. He had a much weaker understanding, and, if possible, a more obstinate temper than his father; that is, more tenacious of opinions he had once formed, though less capable of ever forming right ones. Had he had one grain of merit at the bottom of his heart, one should have had compassion for him in the situation to which his miserable poor head soon reduced him, a mother that despised him, sisters that betrayed him, a brother set up against him, and a set of servants that neglected him, and were neither of use nor capable of being of use to him, or desirous of being so."[34] So said Lord Hervey, and, though his known enmity to Frederick makes one reluctant to accept his estimate, yet it must be admitted that his remarks are borne out by others well qualified to judge. "A poor, weak, irresolute, false, lying, dishonest, contemptible wretch, that nobody loves, that nobody believes, that nobody will trust, and that will trust everybody by turns, and that everybody by turns will impose upon, betray, mislead, and plunder." Thus Sir Robert Walpole, who, during the Prince's lifetime, thought that, if the King should die, the Queen and her unmarried children would be in a bad way. "I do not know any people in the world so much to be pitied," he said to Hervey, "as that gay young company with which you and I stand every day in the drawing-room at that door from which we this moment came, bred up in state, in affluence, caressed and courted, and to go at once from that into dependence upon a brother who loves them not, and whose extravagance and covetousness will make him grudge every guinea they spend, as it must come out of a purse not sufficient to defray the expenses of his own vices."

A later generation has not been more kind. "If," said Leigh Hunt, "George the First was a commonplace man of the quiet order, and George the Second of the bustling, Frederick was of an effeminate sort, pretending to taste and gallantry, and possessed of neither. He affected to patronise literature in order to court popularity, and because his father and grandfather had neglected it;

but he took no real interest in the *literati*, and would meanly stop their pensions when he got out of humour. He passed his time in intriguing against his father, and hastening the ruin of a feeble constitution by sorry amours." "His best quality was generosity," Horace Walpole has recorded; "his worst insincerity and indifference to truth, which appeared so early that Earl Stanhope wrote to Lord Sunderland, 'He has his father's head, and his mother's heart.'"[35]

What is to be said in his favour? That through his intercession Flora Macdonald, imprisoned for harbouring the Chevalier, received her liberty: that when Richard Glover, the author of "Leonidas," fell upon evil days he sent him five hundred pounds; that he was a plausible speaker,[36] fond of music, the author of two songs, and had sufficient sense of humour to institute an occasional practical joke. On the other hand, he was a gambler and a spendthrift without a notion of common honesty; he was unstable and untruthful, a feeble enemy and a lukewarm friend; and is, indeed, best disposed of in the well-known verse:

> "Here lies Fred,
> Who was alive, and is dead.
> Had it been his father,
> I had much rather.
> Had it been his brother,
> Still better than another.
> Had it been his sister,
> No one would have missed her.
> Had it been the whole generation,
> Still better for the nation.
> But since 'tis only Fred,
> Who was alive, and is dead,
> There's no more to be said."

CHAPTER II

BOYHOOD OF GEORGE III

George William Frederick, afterwards George III, was born on June 4, 1738. His advent into the world was so little expected at that time that on the previous day his mother had walked in St. James's Park, had scarcely returned from that exercise when she was taken ill, and between seven and eight o'clock the following morning gave birth to a seven-months' child. Frederick, therefore, could not be held responsible because again no preparation for an *accouchement* had been made, nor could he be blamed because the King had only a few hours' notice of the event.

The baby was so weak that it was thought it would not live, and at eleven o'clock at night it was baptized by the Bishop of Oxford,[37] and though it survived, its health was so delicate that it was thought advisable, and indeed imperative, to abandon the strict court etiquette dictating that a royal infant must be reared by a lady of good family, and instead "the fine, healthy, fresh-coloured wife of a gardener" was chosen. The woman was proud of her charge, but inclined to independence, and when told that, in accordance with tradition, the baby could not sleep with her, "Not sleep with me!" she exclaimed. "Then you may nurse the boy yourselves!" As she remained firm on this point, tradition was wisely cast to the winds, with the fortunate result that the young Prince throve lustily and soon acquired a sound and vigorous frame of body.[38]

It would be to throw away an opportunity for mirth to omit the lines with which Whitehead greeted the birth of a son of the Prince of Wales. These were enthusiastically acclaimed by a contemporary as "a beautiful, prophetic compliment to the future monarch," but the present generation may conceivably find another epithet.

> "Thanks, Nature! thanks! the finish'd piece we own,
> And worthy Frederick's love, and Britain's throne.
> Th' impatient Goddess first had sketch'd the plan,
> Yet ere she durst complete the wond'rous man,
> To try her power, a gentler task design'd,
> And formed a pattern of the softer kind.[39]
> But now, bright boy, thy more exalted ray
> Streams o'er the dawn, and pours a fuller day:
> Nor shall, displeased, to thee her realms resign,
> The earlier promise of the rising line.
> And see! what signs his future worth proclaim,
> See! our *Ascanius* boast a nobler flame!
> On the fair form let vulgar fancies trace
> Some fond presage in ev'ry dawning grace;

More unconfined, poetic transport roves,
Sees all the soul, and all the soul approves:
Sees regal pride but reach the exterior part,
And big with virtues beat the little heart;
Whilst from his eyes soft beams of mercy flow,
And liberty supreme smiles on his infant brow.
Now, in herself secure, shall Albion rise,
And the vain frowns of future fate despise;
See willing worlds beneath her sceptre bend,
And to the verge of Time her fame extend."

Photo by Emery Walker   *From a painting by Richard Wilson*
PRINCE GEORGE OF WALES, PRINCE EDWARD
OF WALES, AND DR. AYSCOUGH

A prince's education begins early, and George was not more than six years of age when he was put into harness. The first tutor selected for him was Dr. Francis Ayscough,[40] whose principal claim to distinction was as brother-in-law to "good Lord Lyttelton," for at best he has been described as a well-meaning but uninspired pedagogue, and at worst, by Walpole, as "an insolent man, unwelcome to the clergy on suspicion of heterodoxy, and of no fair reputation for integrity."[41] Ayscough, as a courtier, was not unsuccessful, for, introduced by Lyttelton[42] and Pitt to Frederick, Prince of Wales, he contrived to ingratiate himself with that invertebrate royal personage; but as an instructor of youth he was not the right man in the right place. He was ignorant of the course to pursue in laying the foundation of a lad's education, and when George was eleven years old, the Princess of Wales found to her dismay her son could not read English, although (so Ayscough assured her) he could make Latin verses. This latter accomplishment could not be accepted as of sufficient importance to excuse ignorance of more practical subjects, and a new preceptor, George Scott, was introduced on the recommendation of Lord Bolingbroke, who, Walpole states significantly, "had lately seen the Prince two or three times in private." This appointment marks the beginning of the intrigues that centred round the young Prince.

Tempted by the promise of an earldom, in October, 1750, Lord North [43] became Governor—"an amiable, worthy man," says Walpole, "of no great genius, unless compared with his successor;" but this arrangement did not long endure, for the Pelhams, finding themselves in power, thought it behoved them to endeavour to retain it perpetually by surrounding the future king with their creatures. Lord North retired in April, 1751, and, when the post had been offered to and declined by Lord Hartington, he was replaced by Lord Harcourt,[44] a Lord of the Bedchamber to the King, a "civil and stupid" person who, though unfitted for the post by his ignorance of most things save hunting and drinking, was thought unlikely to interfere with the ministers' plans. The real agent of the Pelhams was the sub-governor, Andrew Stone,[45] the Duke of Newcastle's private secretary, "a dark, proud man, very able and very mercenary," in high favour with George II. Scott remained as Sub-Preceptor, and with him as Preceptor was now put Dr. Hayter, Bishop of Norwich,[46] a sensible man of the world. Lord Sussex, Lord Robert Bertie, and Lord Downe were appointed Lords, and Peachy, Digby and Schulze, Grooms of the Bedchamber to the young Prince; while his Treasurer was Colonel John Selwyn, who, dying in December, was succeeded by Cresset, the holder of the same position in the Household of the Princess, now Dowager Princess of Wales.

For a while there was peace in the tutors' camp, but soon dissension broke out, and it became an open secret that Harcourt and Hayter were in opposition to Stone and Scott. The quarrel began when Hayter found in the Prince of Wales's hands a copy of Father d'Orleans's *"Revolution d'Angleterre,"* a work written at the instigation of James II of England to justify his measures. Stone was taxed with having introduced it into the royal apartments, when he denied ever having seen it in thirty years, and expressed his willingness to stand or fall by the truth or falseness of the accusation; but when Hayter showed a desire to take him at his word, it was admitted that the Prince had the book, and the defence set up was that Prince Edward had borrowed it of his sister Augusta. Then other works not suitable for use in the training of a constitutional monarch were, it is said, discovered to be in the possession of the Prince; and though Stone and Scott aped humility and regret, they contrived notwithstanding to irritate their superior officers, until one day Hayter lost his temper, and removed Scott from the royal chamber "by an imposition of hands, that had at least as much of the flesh as the spirit in the force of the action."[47] When matters came to this pass, Cresset took a hand in the quarrel, and finally Murray[48] added fuel to the flame by telling the Bishop that Stone should be shown more consideration. Hayter replied, "He believed that Mr. Stone found all proper regard, but that Lord Harcourt, the chief of the trust, was generally present;" to which Murray retorted, "Lord Harcourt, pho! he is a cypher, and must be a cypher, and was put in to be a cypher." That was the last straw. There are men who are cyphers without knowing it, and men who know they are cyphers and do not resent their unimportance, but there are few who can with impunity be told that they are cyphers, and of these Harcourt was not one, for, with all his faults, he was not the man to acquiesce in the use of himself as a cat's-paw.

When the King returned in November, 1752, from Hanover, Harcourt complained that dangerous and arbitrary principles were being instilled into the Prince, and stated it was useless for him to remain as Governor unless those who were misleading the lad were removed from their official positions about his person. A few days after this protest was registered, the Archbishop of Canterbury and the Lord Chancellor sent word that by the King's command they would wait on Lord Harcourt for further particulars of his grievance, but the latter declined to receive them on the ground that, "His complaints were not proper to be told but to the King himself." At a private interview with George II on December 6, Harcourt tendered his resignation, which was accepted; but a similar concession was not granted to the Bishop of Norwich, whose resignation the King preferred to receive through the medium of the Archbishop of Canterbury.[49]

From an old print
AUGUSTA, PRINCESS DOWAGER OF WALES

The position of the Governor and Preceptor had gradually become untenable, for they were exposed to the cross-influences of the Princess Dowager of Wales and the ministers, and, in their efforts to secure for themselves the favour of their charge, they took no trouble to win the good graces of the Princess or to live at peace with their subordinates. "The Bishop, thinking himself already minister to the future King, expected dependence from, never once thought of depending upon, the inferior governors. In the education of the two Princes, he was sincerely honest and zealous; and soon grew to thwart the Princess whenever, as an indulgent, or perhaps a little as an ambitious mother (and this happened but too frequently), she was willing to relax the application of her sons. Lord Harcourt was minute and strict in trifles; and thinking that he discharged his trust conscientiously if on no account he neglected to make the Prince turn out his toes, he gave himself little trouble to respect the Princess, or to condescend to the Sub-governor."[50] To this testimony must be added that of Bubb Dodington, who declared that Lord Harcourt not only behaved ill to the Princess Dowager and spoke to the children of their dead father in a manner most disrespectful, but also did all in his power to alienate them from their mother. "George," he says, "had mentioned it once since Lord Harcourt's departure, that he was afraid he had not behaved as well to her sometimes as he ought, and wondered how he could be so misled."[51] The Princess was therefore overjoyed to be rid of Lord Harcourt, not only for these reasons, but for another that will presently be discussed.

Stone and Scott retained their posts, but it was not found easy to replace the men who had resigned. Ministers desired to appoint as Preceptor Dr. Johnson, [52] the new Bishop of Gloucester, but the Whigs were so bitterly opposed to the nomination, and had the support of the Archbishop's objections, that eventually Dr. Thomas[53] was given the office. "It was still more difficult to accommodate themselves with a Governor," Walpole has recorded. "The post was at once too exalted, and they had declared it too unsubstantial, to leave it easy to find a man who could fill the honour, and digest the dishonour of it."[54] Overtures were made in several quarters but without success, until at last, at the request of the King, Lord Waldegrave[55] consented to accept the responsibility. This he did only after "repeated assurances of the submission and tractability of Stone," and then with great reluctance, for he was a man of pleasure rather than of affairs, and reluctant to be embroiled in intrigue. "If I dared," he said to a friend, "I would make this excuse to the King, 'Sir, I am too young to govern, and too old to be governed.'" Even this appointment was censured by the Whigs, for, though Waldegrave was a man of great common sense and undoubted honour, it was objected that "his grandmother was a daughter of King James; his family were all Papists, and his father had been but the first convert"!

The refusal of Lord Harcourt to discuss his complaints with any one but the King was doubtless due to the fact that he traced the objectionable doctrines taught to his pupil to Lord Bute.[56] In his earlier years Bute had taken no part nor, indeed, shown any interest in politics. In 1723, at the age of twenty, he had succeeded to the earldom on the death of his father; had married Mary, only daughter of Lady Mary Wortley Montagu, and so came into possession of the Wortley estates; and, though in 1737 elected representative peer of Scotland, had spent most of his time on his estates, occupying himself with the theoretical and practical study of agriculture and architecture.

A great change in Bute's life was made in 1747 through a chance meeting with Frederick, Prince of Wales. The Earl was then staying at Richmond, and one day his neighbour, an apothecary, drove him over to Moulsey Hurst to see a cricket match that had been organized by the Prince. It came on to rain, the game had to be stopped, and Frederick retired to his tent, proposing a rubber of whist to while away the time until the weather should clear. Only two other players could be found, but some one espied Bute in the carriage and, learning that he could play, invited him to make up the table. The Prince, who had never before met him, was charmed with his manners, and invited him to Kew. "How often do great events arise from trifling causes," exclaims the worthy but sententious Seward. "An apothecary keeping his carriage may have occasioned the Peace of Paris, the American War, and the National Assembly in France." Without going so far as that chronicler, it may be said that the game of whist had far-reaching effects.

From a print published 1754 for "Stowe's Survey"
LEICESTER HOUSE

Bute became a member of his patron's court,[57] where his influence became a factor that could not be ignored. Nor did his power at Leicester House wane after the death of the Prince, for he was high in the Princess's favour, which latter good fortune was attributed not so much to his intellectual attainments as to his personal qualities. Scandal was busy coupling his name with that of the lady he served: indeed, for years there was no caricature so popular with the public as that of the Boot and the Petticoat, the symbols of the Peer and the Princess. What truth there was in this charge, if, indeed, there was any truth at all, is not, and probably never will be, known; but at the time the intimacy was almost universally assumed. "It had already been whispered that the assiduities of Lord Bute at Leicester House, and his still more frequent attendance in the gardens at Kew and Carlton House, were less addressed to the Prince of Wales than to his mother," says Walpole. "The eagerness of the pages of the back-stairs to let her know whenever Lord Bute arrived (and some other symptoms) contributed to dispel the ideas that had been conceived of the rigour of her widowhood. On the other hand, the favoured personage, naturally ostentatious of his person, and of haughty carriage, seemed by no means desirous of concealing his conquest. His bows grew more theatric; his graces contracted some meaning; and the beauty of his leg was constantly displayed in the eye of the poor captivated Princess.... When the late Prince of Wales affected to retire into gloomy *allées* with Lady Middleton, he used to bid the Princess walk with Lord Bute. As soon as the Prince was dead, they walked more and more, in honour of his memory."[58] The same authority was on another occasion even more explicit. "I am as much convinced of the amorous connexion between Bute and the Princess Dowager as if I had seen them together," he said;[59] and what he said was thought by the more reticent.

Whether there was "amorous connexion" or not, Bute was the most detested man of his day, and the more prominently he came before the public the more violent was the abuse heaped upon him. "Bute was hated with a rage of which there have been few examples in English history. He was the butt for everybody's abuse; for Wilkes's devilish mischief; for Churchill's slashing satire; for the hooting of the mob that roasted the boot, his emblem, in a thousand bonfires; that hated him because he was a favourite and a Scotchman, calling him 'Mortimer,' 'Lothario,' I know not what names, and accusing his royal mistress of all sorts of crimes—the grave, lean, demure, elderly woman, who, I daresay, was quite as good as her neighbours."[60]

In those days to be a Scotchman was alone enough to secure the cordial ill-will of the English, for national rivalries had not then been even partially eliminated; and it was said that Bute used his power to promote his countrymen, which, though to-day it does not seem a very heinous crime, was then regarded as a sin unequalled in horror by any enumerated in the decalogue. An amusing defence of Bute against this charge is made by Huish who, however, was certainly unconscious of the humour of the passage. "The truth of this charge rests upon no solid foundation. That Bute brought forward his countrymen is true enough, but it was by extending to them the patronage of office, not, except in some few instances, by directly introducing them to the personal favour of the King."[61] One of these exceptions was Charles Jenkinson,[62] Bute's private secretary, who, when his master had, ostensibly, at least, retired from the direction of affairs, was the go between the King and the ex-minister.

"Lord Bute was my schoolfellow," says Walpole. "He was a man of taste and science, and I do believe his intentions were good. He wished to blend and unite all parties. The Tories were willing to come in for a *share* of power, after having been so long excluded—but the Whigs were not willing to grant that share. Power is an intoxicating draught; the more a man has, the more he desires."[63] The effects of power upon Bute will soon appear. It was not, however, this man's power or his use or abuse of it, but his qualities, that earned for him the hatred of his equals. Lord Chesterfield wrote him down as "dry, unconciliatory, and sullen, with a great mixture of pride. He never looked at those he spoke to, or who spoke to him, a great fault in a minister, as in the general opinion of mankind it implies conscious guilt; besides that it hinders him from penetrating others.... He was too proud to be respectable or respected; too cold and silent to be amiable; too cunning to have great abilities; and his inexperience made him too precipitately what it disabled him from executing."[64] Further, he showed little *savoir faire*, for he chose as his subordinates, men who were incapable, or those who, disgusted by him, were undesirous to help him, and, giving no man his confidence, found himself severely handicapped consequently by receiving none. Indeed, his arrogance on occasion angered even the Prince of Wales, who quarrelled with him before the death of George II, and on his accession employed him only after the severest pressure of the Princess Dowager.[65] However, Bute soon regained his ascendency over the young King.

One result of the intimacy between the Princess Dowager and Bute was that the actual superintendence, and, indeed, control of the education of the Prince of Wales was indirectly exercised by him. This was particularly unfortunate because Bute was a disciple of Bolingbroke's doctrine of absolute monarchy, and his "high prerogative prejudice and Tory predilections," similar to those that caused the Revolution of 1688, were specially dangerous at a time when the new dynasty had not long been firmly established; and it seemed that while at worst they might lead to a conflict between the Crown and the people, at best they would, when the Prince of Wales became King, make Bute a dictator. Even so early as 1752 Waldegrave "found his Royal Highness full of princely prejudices, contracted in the nursing, and improved by the society of bed-chamber women, and the pages of the back-stairs,"[66] and he records the endeavours to make him resign his Governorship so that the place might be open for Bute.

"A notion has prevailed," says Nicholls, "that the Earl of Bute had suggested political opinions to the Princess Dowager, but this was certainly a mistake. In understanding, the Princess Dowager was far superior to the Earl of Bute; in whatever degree of favour he stood with her, he did not suggest, but he received, her opinions and her directions."[67] As a matter of fact, the Princess Dowager was a woman of very sound understanding up to a certain point, but her training at the Court of Saxe-Gotha, where the Duke was practically a despot, unfitted her for the task of bringing up a future King of England. Constitutional monarchy was beyond the range of her experience, and she could never accept the doctrine in force in this country that, while a sovereign may choose his ministers, having chosen them he should either be guided by their advice or change them. "Be a King, George," she preached to the heir-apparent; and in her eyes to be a king was to be omnipotent.

Though well-meaning and shrewd enough, the Princess Dowager's outlook on life was narrow; she had many prejudices, and in the light of these planned the education of her children so far as it lay in her power. She was so afraid lest George should be influenced by the vulgarity and immorality of the Court, that she tied him to her apron-strings. "The Prince of Wales lived shut up with his mother and Lord Bute; and must have thrown them into some difficulties: their connexion was not easily reconcilable to the devotion which they had infused into the Prince; the Princess could not wish him always present, and yet dreaded him being out of her sight. His brother Edward, who received a thousand mortifications, was seldom suffered to be with him; and Lady Augusta, now a woman, was, to facilitate some privacy for the Princess, dismissed from supping with her mother, and sent back to cheese-cakes, with her little sister Elizabeth, on pretence that meat at night would fatten her too much."[68] The result of this treatment was not only that the children were miserable, but that they were all too well aware of their state of mind. When the Princess Dowager, struck one day by the silence of one of her sons, asked if he were sulking, "I was thinking," the lad replied, "what I should feel if I had a son as unhappy as you make me."

There were not wanting those who declared that in secluding the Prince of Wales, and in keeping from him all knowledge of the world—that knowledge, valuable to all, but essential to the making of a useful King—the Princess Dowager had formed the project herself to exercise the regal power that would one day be his; and that her policy was approved by Lord Bute, who, also with an eye to the future, saw that his influence over an ignorant monarch was likely to be much greater than over one well acquainted with men and matters. "The plan of tutelage and future dominion over the heir-apparent, laid many years ago at Carlton House, between the Princess Dowager and her favourite, the Earl of Bute, was as gross and palpable as that which was concerted between Anne of Austria and Cardinal Mazarin, to govern Lewis the Fourteenth, and in effect to prolong his minority until the end of their lives. That Prince had strong natural parts, and used frequently to blush for his own ignorance and want of education, which had been wilfully neglected by his mother and her minion. A little experience, however, soon showed him how shamefully he had been treated, and for what infamous purposes he had been kept in ignorance. Our great Edward, too, at an early period, had sense enough to understand the nature of the connexion between his abandoned mother and the detested Mortimer. But since that time human nature, we may observe, is greatly altered for the better. Dowagers may be chaste, and minions may be honest. When it was proposed to settle the present King's household as Prince of Wales, it is well known that the Earl of Bute was forced into it in direct contradiction to the late King's inclination. *That* was the salient point from which all the mischiefs and disgraces of the present reign took life and motion. From that moment Lord Bute never suffered the Prince of Wales to be an instant out of his sight. We need not look farther."[69]

But while the Princess Dowager and Lord Bute agreed apparently as to the advantage of keeping the heir-apparent in a backward state, each desiring the mastery, they differed on other points. "The Princess began to perceive an alteration in the ardour of Lord Bute, which grew less assiduous about her, and increased towards her son," Walpole noted in 1758. "The Earl had attained such an ascendency over the Prince, that he became more remiss to the mother; and no doubt it was an easier function to lead the understanding of a youth than to keep up to the spirit required by an experienced woman. The Prince even dropped hints against women interfering in politics. These clouds, however, did not burst; and the creatures of the Princess vindicated her from any breach with Lord Bute with as much earnestness as if their union had been to her honour."[70]

The Princess did not deny that the seclusion of her son had its drawbacks. "She was highly sensible how necessary it was that the Prince should keep company with men: she well knew that women could not inform him, but if it was in her power absolutely, to whom could she entrust him? What company could she wish him to keep? What friendships desire he should contract? Such was the universal profligacy, such the character and conduct of the young people of distinction, that she was really afraid to have them near her children." However, the Princess Dowager made little or no effort to provide suitable companions for George, and the only youth with whom he was allowed to have even a restricted intercourse was his brother, Edward.

From a painting by H. Kysing
GEORGE, PRINCE OF WALES

Frederick, Prince of Wales, had not set his wife a good example by showing much interest in his son, though when he was on his deathbed he sent for the child. "Come, George," he said, "let us be good friends while we may." Occasionally, however, he had gone with him to a concert at the Foundling Hospital, or to see various processes of manufactures; and now and then had taken him for a walk in the city at night—which latter proceeding gave rise to a lampoon when in 1749 the little boy was installed a Knight of the Garter,—the Earl of Inchiquin appearing as his proxy.

> "Now Frederick's a knight and George is a knight,
>   With stalls in Windsor Chapel,
> We'll hope they'll prowl no more by night,
>   To look at garters black and white,
>   On legs of female rabble."

On the death of his father, George succeeded to the title of Electoral Prince of Brunswick-Lünenburg, Duke of Edinburgh, Marquis of the Isle of Ely, Earl of Eltham, Viscount of Launceston and Baron of Snowdon; and the "Gazette" of April 11, 1751, announced that, "His Majesty had been pleased to order Letters Patent to pass under the Great Seal of Great Britain for creating his Royal Highness George William Frederick ... Prince of Wales and Earl of Chester." George II at this time began to show a personal interest in his successor, inviting him to St. James's, taking him to Kew, even for a while removing him from Leicester House and lodging him at Kensington. The King did not approve of his daughter-in-law's method of bringing up her son, and, when visiting her unexpectedly one day, heard she had taken the Princes to visit a tapestry factory in which she was interested. "D——n dat tapestry," he cried, "I shall have de Princes made women of." Calling again at Leicester House the next day, he inquired: "Gone to de tapestry again?" and, on being told the Princes were at home, commanded that they should be sent to Hyde Park where he had "oder things to show dem dan needles and dreads." The "oder things" was a review, and, Princess Augusta being dressed to go out, her grandfather took her with him. "This circumstance gave rise to some unpleasant altercation between the King and the Princess Dowager of Wales; for, on the latter being informed of the expressions which his Majesty had used regarding her visit to the tapestry manufactory, she retorted upon his Majesty by declaring if he thought the view of a manufactory was beneath the attentions of her sons, she considered the sight of a review to be attended with no benefit to her daughter."[71]

The Princess Dowager's retort to the King in this case was typical of her character, for she was a strong-minded, fearless woman, and not lightly to be brow-beaten or opposed.[72] On the whole, however, George II and his daughter-in-law were not on unfriendly terms since, after the death of her husband, she had thrown herself upon his protection. "The King and she both took their parts at once," Walpole noted; "she of flinging herself entirely into his hands and studying nothing but his pleasure, but with wondering what interest she got with him to the advantage of her son and the Prince's friends; the King of acting the tender grandfather, which he, who had never acted the tender father, grew so pleased with representing, that he soon became it in earnest." This was made clear when the question arose of appointing a regent in case of the sovereign's death before his successor was of age, for the King advocated her right to be selected for that exalted position in a Royal Message to the Houses of Parliament:

"That nothing could conduce so much to the preservation of the Protestant succession in his royal family as proper provision for the tuition of the person of his successor, and for the regular administration of the government, in case the successor should be of tender years: his Majesty, therefore, earnestly recommended this weighty affair to the deliberation of Parliament and proposed that when the imperial crown of these realms should descend to any of the late Prince's sons, being under the age of eighteen years, his mother, the Princess Dowager of Wales, should be guardian of his person, and Regent of these kingdoms, until he should attain the age of majority; with such powers and limitations as should appear necessary and expedient for these purposes."

A Bill embodying these recommendations was accordingly introduced by the Duke of Newcastle into the House of Lords, when the King sent a second Message proposing that such a council to assist the Regent as the Bill advised should consist of the Duke of Cumberland, then Commander-in-Chief, the Archbishop of Canterbury, the Lord Chancellor, the Lord High Treasurer, or First Lord Commissioner of the Treasury, the President of the Council, the Lord Privy Seal, the Lord High Admiral of Great Britain, or First Commissioner of the Admiralty, the two principal Secretaries of State, and the Lord Chief Justice of the King's Bench—all those great officers except, of course, the Duke of Cumberland, for the time being.

This aroused the bitterest opposition, and many members dwelt on the danger of leaving in command of a large standing army a prince of the blood, who was the only permanent member of the Council as well as the uncle of the minor, and the names of all the wicked uncles in history, John Lackland, Humphrey of Gloucester, and the rest were freely introduced into the discussion. William Augustus Duke of Cumberland, was indeed a deeply hated man, and the astonishing popularity of his elder brother, Frederick, was perhaps due more to the fact that he stood between William and the throne than to any other reason. Indeed, when Frederick died, in many cases the lament was phrased "Would that it had been his brother!" "Would that it had been 'the butcher!'" and Walpole is careful to mention that the nickname was not given in the sense it was formerly: "*Le boucher étoit anciennement un surnom glorieux qu'on donnoit à un general àpres une victoire, en reconnoissance du carnage qu'il avoit fait de trente ou quarante mille hommes.*"[73] Yet, "there never was a prince so popular, so winning in his ways, as William of Cumberland during his minority," says Dr. Doran, who adds that "*the* Duke," as he was called, was "gentlemanlike without affectations, accomplished without being vain of his accomplishments."[74]

He had courage in plenty, and distinguished himself at Dettingen and Culloden, but his severities after the latter battle secured him the undesirable nickname that clung to him for life—in his defence it may be offered that this same harshness might well have earned for him the gratitude of those who hated civil war, for it scotched further rebellion and made his father's throne secure. He had hoped to be appointed regent, although Walpole tells us "the consternation that spread on the apprehensions that the Duke would be regent on the King's death, and have the sole power in the meantime, was near as strong as what was occasioned by the notice of the rebels being at Derby."[75] None the less, when the Lord Chancellor was sent to inform him that his hope would not be realized, the Duke bore the blow well, and said, "I return my duty and thanks to the King for the communication of the plan of regency; while, for the post allotted to me, I would submit to it, because he commands it, be that regency what it will." He felt resentful, however, wished "the name of William could be blotted out of the English annals," and declared he now felt his insignificance, "when even Mr. Pelham would dare to use him thus." The opposition to the inclusion of his name even on the council to assist the regent gave him pain; but he was much more deeply wounded when, the young Prince of Wales calling upon him, to amuse his visitor he took down a sword and drew it, and noticed that the lad turned pale and trembled. "What must they have told him about me," he wondered, and in no measured terms complained to the Princess of Wales of the impression that had been instilled into his nephew.

CHAPTER III

THE PRINCE COMES OF AGE

"The boy is good for nothing but to read the Bible to his mother," George II said one day of his grandson; and he sought for measures that should emancipate the young man and tend to enlarge his knowledge of the world. His first attempt in this direction, made in 1755 when he was in Hanover, fluttered the dovecots of Leicester House, for the rumour flew that the King was about to propose a marriage between the Prince of Wales and a princess of the House of Brunswick. "Surely the King would not marry my son without acquainting me with it, so much as by letter," said the Princess Dowager. "If the King should settle the match without acquainting me, I should let him know how ill I take it, and I shall not fail to tell him fairly and plainly it is full early." The report proved to be not unfounded. At a German watering-place, George II had met the Duchess of Brunswick with her two daughters, and had been so charmed with the elder, Sophia,[76] that he declared if he had been twenty years younger he would have married her himself.

From a portrait by T. Frye

GEORGE III

When the King's wish became known to the Princess Dowager, she determined by every means in her power to thwart it, and as a first step told her son that his grandfather's only motive in proposing the marriage was to advance the interest of Hanover. "The suddenness of the measure, and the little time left for preventing it, at once unhinged all the circumspection and prudence of the Princess. From the death of the Prince, her object had been the government of her son; and her attention had answered. She had taught him great devotion, and she had taken care he should be taught nothing else. There was no reason to apprehend from his own genius that he would escape her, but bigoted, and young, and chaste, what empire might not a youthful bride (and the Princess of Brunswick was reckoned artful) assume over him? The Princess thought that prudence now would be most imprudent. She immediately instilled into her son the greatest aversion to the match: he protested against it."[77] Every artifice was employed by the Princess Dowager and Bute to prejudice the Prince of Wales against Princess Sophia, her personal attractions were depreciated, and she was represented as the last person in the world likely to render the married state acceptable, while on the other hand, "the charms, the mental qualifications, the superior endowments, and the fascinating manners of a princess of a house of Saxe-Gotha were the constant theme of panegyric, the diamond could not surpass her eye in brilliancy, nor the snow the whiteness of her skin." These descriptions fired even the Prince, who refused the King's nominee, and made formal demands for a portrait of the Saxe-Gotha beauty—a request that in royal circles is usually the first step towards an alliance. Of course his grandson's action became known to the King, who would not entertain the idea of his successor's union with a princess of the Saxe-Gotha blood, which was notorious for a constitutional malady. "I know enough of that family already," he said, and no arguments could move him.

This, of course, put an end to the negotiations, but the Prince of Wales, incensed, it was said, by the affront to his mother's family, replied by refusing even to discuss any other alliance. "In vain his Majesty importuned him; in vain the most serious and plausible representations were made to him of the necessity of his marriage as an act of state policy; in vain were all the arguments adduced which had been so satisfactorily employed in the discussion of the Regency Bill, concerning the danger which impends over the country, when the monarch or the heir-apparent to the throne marries at a late period of his life, thereby giving rise to the probability of a long minority: in vain the character of the patriot prince was exposed to him, who ought to sacrifice his private feelings to the welfare of the state. To all these powerful and cogent reasons he granted a willing and respectful ear, and an hour's private conversation with his mother effaced every impression which they had made."[78]

When the King's project for the marriage of his successor fell through, the ministers made an effort on their own account to withdraw the Prince of Wales from the maternal influence, being thereto incited by the fact that a bid for the young man's sympathies were being made by the Opposition and that at his informal *levées* Pitt, Lord Temple,[79] and the Grenvilles[80] were frequently in attendance. The Duke of Newcastle[81] and Lord Hardwicke[82], who also desired the favour of the future sovereign, took alarm, and endeavoured, with a single diplomatic stroke, to checkmate Pitt and his friends and separate mother and son. Lord Waldegrave was sent by the King, at the instance of the ministers, to state that now the Prince of Wales had attained the year of royal majority, his Majesty would allow him £40,000 a year, and had given orders to prepare for him Frederick's apartments at Kensington and those of the late Queen at Kew. Upon receipt of this message a secret conclave was held at Leicester House, and, as a result, the Prince sent a reply, probably drawn up by Legge, that he would gratefully accept the allowance, but preferred not to leave his mother.

As the latter proposal had not been made a condition of the grant, ministers were non-plussed. "Was the gift to be revoked, because the Prince had natural affection? Was the whole message to be carried into execution, and a young man, of age by Act of Parliament, to be taken by force, and detained a prisoner in the palace? What law would justify such violence? Who would be the agents of such violence? His Majesty himself and the late Prince of Wales had furnished the Prince with precedents of mutinying against the crown with impunity. How little the ministers, who had planned the first step, knew what to advise for the second, was plain, from their giving no further advice for about a month, and from the advice which they did give then, and from the perplexity in which they remained for two months more, and from the ignominious result of the whole transaction, both to the King and to themselves at last."[83]

The King's offer had been made at the end of May or the beginning of June, 1756, and the Prince of Wales, acting under his mother's instructions, had followed up his second victory by carrying the war into the enemy's camp, and expressing a desire that Lord Bute should be appointed his Groom of the Stole. In July a second message in the King's name was sent to the heir-apparent to inquire if he still adhered to his desire to remain with his mother and to the demand for the appointment of Lord Bute. This, intended as a warning or threat, failed of its intended effect, for the Prince replied: "That since the King did him the honour to ask him the question, he did hope to have leave to continue with his mother, as her happiness so much depended on it—for the other point, he had *never directly* asked it—yet, since encouraged, he would explain himself; and from the long knowledge and good opinion he had of Lord Bute, he did desire to have him about his person."

After this, there was nothing for it but surrender on the part of the ministers, who could not but admit to themselves that they had played the game and lost it. Lord Waldegrave was relieved from the post of Governor, much to his pleasure, for he had found his servitude uncongenial; and to the delight of the Princess Dowager, who had unreasonably regarded him as a spy, and also of the Prince of Wales, who had no liking for him, and subsequently denounced him as "a depraved, worthless man, well-intentioned, but wholly unfit for the situation in which he was placed." The King accepted Lord Waldegrave's resignation with regret; and consented to bestow the gold key on Lord Bute only with great reluctance—indeed, so strong was his feeling in the matter that he refused to give the insignia of office himself as was usual, and sent it by the Duke of Grafton, who slipped it into the pocket of the recipient, and advised him to show no offence.

Bute kissed hands as Groom of the Stole in October, at the same time as the other members of the Prince of Wales's new establishment, in which Lord Huntingdon was Master of the Horse, Lord Euston, Lord Pembroke, and Lord Digby, Lords of the Bedchamber; Lord Bathurst, treasurer; Hon. S. Masham, Auditor; and Hon. James Brudenel, Master of the Robes. Andrew Stone was appointed Secretary, and his first duty was to carry out his master's wish that George Scott should not be retained in the Household. "The reason given for his exclusion was, his having talked with contempt of the Prince's understanding, and with freedom of the Princess's conduct. The truth was, Scott was a frank man, of no courtly depth, and had indiscreetly disputed with Lord Bute, who affected a character of learning."[84] This prejudice was unfortunate, for, according to Rose, Scott, though no courtier, was the sort of man who should have been kept by George about his person. "I never knew a man more entirely blameless in all the relations of life; amiable, honourable, temperate, and one of the sweetest dispositions I ever knew."[85] But he was too clear-sighted to be a welcome person in court circles and his lack of deference to the fetish set up by the Princess Dowager was in her eyes unpardonable.

From the appointment of his Household in 1856 so uneventful was the life of the Prince of Wales that there is nothing to record of the years intervening until he ascended the throne, to which he was called suddenly. On October 25, 1760, George II rose at the usual hour, seemingly in good health; but, as the page left the room after breakfast, he heard a noise, and found the King had fallen from his chair to the floor. "Call Amelia," said the monarch; and instantly expired.

Photo by Emery Walker   *Portrait by Allan Ramsay*
GEORGE III IN HIS CORONATION ROBES

CHAPTER IV

THE NEW KING

The King is dead! Long live the King!

George II has given place to George III, and those who had prostrated themselves before the former were now anxious to pay court to his successor. Yet those who had at heart the welfare of their country trembled at the thought that the throne, with all the influence appertaining thereto, had passed to an ignorant, narrow-minded lad; and reviewing the young king's training, and his mediocre gifts, it must be admitted that the fear was not unreasonable.

The Princess Dowager's plan of isolating the Prince of Wales from companions of his own age, while it had kept him from evil counsellors, had resulted only too obviously in making him a very dull young man. His mother admitted he was "shy and backward; not a wild dissipated boy, but good-natured and cheerful, with a serious cast upon the whole;"[86] and unfortunately the mode of life imposed upon him during his minority tended to develop that serious cast at the expense of other qualities. Bubb Dodington, a keen observer, noticed this trait so early as 1752, and asked the Princess Dowager what she thought the real disposition of the Prince to be. "She said that I knew him almost as well as she did; that he was very honest, but she wished that he was a little more forward, and less childish at his age: that she hoped his preceptors would improve him. I begged to know what methods they took; what they read to him, or made him read; and whether he showed any particular inclination to any of the people about him. She said she did not well know what they taught him; but, to speak freely, she was afraid not much: that they were in the country and followed their diversions, and not much else that she could discover: that we must hope it would be better when we came to town. I said that I did not much regard books, that what I the most wished was that his Royal Highness should begin to learn the usages and knowledge of the world; be informed of the general frame and nature of this government and constitution, and of the general course and manner of business, without descending into minutias."[87]

The young Prince of Wales's amusements had been few. He was sometimes permitted to play a round card game, called Comet, with his mother and brothers and sisters; and the Princess Dowager showed more liberality of mind than was usual with her by declaring that "she liked the Prince should now and then amuse himself at small play, but that princes should never play deep, both for the example and because it did not become them to win great sums."[88] A greater delight of the Prince was to take part in amateur theatricals, an indulgence sometimes granted as the practice might accustom him to the public speaking that must later fall to his lot. This was of great value to him for, while in conversation his utterance was rapid, on public occasions he spoke so distinctly and with such dignity that Quin, hearing his first Speech from the throne, exclaimed delightedly: "Ay! 'twas I that taught the boy to speak!" But George was not fond of delivering or listening to orations. "I am sure that the rage for public speaking, and the extravagant length to which some of our more popular orators carry their harangues in Parliament, is very detrimental to the national business," he expressed his opinion after he ascended the throne, "and I wish that it may not, in the end, prove injurious to the public peace."[89]

In spite of these occasional relaxations, the family circle at Leicester House was far from bright, and Dodington has recorded how in November, 1753, he was summoned to wait upon the Princess Dowager, and how, instead of the small party and a little music he expected, he found no one but her Royal Highness, the Prince of Wales, Prince Edward and Princess Augusta, all in undress. They sat round the fire, and Dodington and the Princess talked of familiar occurrences "with the ease and unreservedness and unconstraint, as if one had dropped into a sister's house that had a family, to pass the evening," but agreeable as it was to Dodington, he could not refrain from wishing, "that the Princess conversed familiarly with more people of a certain knowledge of the world."[90] But even Dodington seldom saw the Prince of Wales, and, though George II showed no disposition to keep his successor in the background, the latter spent much of his time in, perhaps not entirely voluntary, retirement at Kew, where his mother was making "a collection of exotic plants, the precursor of the present Royal Botanical Gardens, on a scale of liberal munificence, besides continuing to erect, under the superintendence of Sir William Chambers, the various ornamental gardens, originally planned by the deceased Prince."[91] Horticulture had little charm for the Prince of Wales, who was, however, attracted by agricultural science, and took an active interest in the farming of his land, tastes which subsequently he endeavoured in vain to inculcate in his sons, and secured for him the nickname that still clings to him.[92]

From the Oxford Magazine
THE BUTTON MAKER

George found some pleasure in trifling mechanical occupations, and had a watch made from his own designs by Arnold, of which a description is extant. "It was rather less than a silver twopence, yet contained one hundred and twenty different parts: the whole weighed between five and six pennyweights." Later in life he amused himself in turning on the lathe, and it was declared by the satirists that the royal ingenuity eventually went so far as to construct a button. Certainly for a long time he figured in caricature as "the royal button-maker"; and it was in this capacity an anonymous versifier congratulated him upon the success of his army in America.

> "Then shall my lofty numbers tell
> Who taught the royal babes to spell
> And sovereign art pursue
> To mend a watch, or set a clock,
> New pattern shape for Hervey's frock,
> Or buttons made at Kew."[93]

George III as Prince of Wales saw nothing of the outside world, and even when in 1759 he was allowed to make an excursion beyond the limits usually imposed upon him, it took the form of a private trip through Scotland, when, preserving the strictest *incognito*, he paid visits to Edinburgh, Glasgow, the Isle of Bute and a few other places, accompanied only by Lord Bute and two servants.

It may here be remarked that no English king travelled less than George III, who during the whole of his long life rarely visited any part of his dominions.

> "Our sons some slave of greatness may behold,
> Cast in the genuine Asiatic mould,

> Who of three realms shall condescend to know
> No more than he can spy from Windsor's brow."[94]

He never went to Hanover or Scotland or Ireland or Wales, and in England his longest journeys were to Cheltenham, Weymouth, and Portsmouth, which latter town he visited twice, but solely to make an official inspection of a battleship.

> "There shall he see, as other folks have seen,
> That ships have anchors, and that seas are green;
> Shall count the tackling trim, the streamers fine,
> With Bradshaw prattle, and with Sandwich dine;
> And then row back, amidst the cannon's roar,
> As safe, as sage, as when he left the shore."[95]

"To tell you the honest truth," Ernest, King of Hanover, said in 1845; "the impression on my mind has ever been that it was a very unfortunate circumstance for my father that he was kept as it were, aloof, not only from his brothers, but almost from all young men of his own age; and this I saw evident marks of almost daily."[96] Indeed, the unhappy relations of George III with his sons must in great part be attributed to the isolation of the King's early years: never having been permitted to indulge in the pleasures of youth, he could in later years make no allowance for such follies in others. It comes as a relief to find that George III when Prince of Wales did commit one stupid, boyish prank: when a tutor reproved him and told him he must stick closer to his work, he put pitch on the tutor's chair, thus making the pedagogue stick closer to his seat.

Some lads who, from one cause or another, see little society, derive knowledge of the world from books, but George was not one of these. He did not learn easily, and he had not been helped by an extensive or thorough education. His knowledge of Latin or Greek was negligible, and Huish's statement that at an early age the Prince "correctly understood the history of modern times and the just relations of England with the other states" makes too great a strain upon our credulity. It is true that in support of his view Huish prints a list of titles of plays that the Prince is said to have selected to show the condition of various states and persons; but though, as a matter of fact this has little to recommend it as an intellectual exercise, it is unlikely the youth performed even this task without assistance.[97] It may be conceded, however, that he read with more or less understanding the history of England, France and Germany; and that he could speak the language of these countries with fluency. He wrote English with little show of acquaintance with grammar and never could spell correctly, while his general knowledge was lamentably slight, and in spite of fulsome biographers, books never had any attraction for him. "He never delighted in study, nor ever passed much of his time in sedentary occupations, calculated to improve his mind, after his accession to the crown," Wraxall admits frankly. "A newspaper which he commonly took up after dinner, and over which, however interesting its contents might be, he usually fell asleep in less than half-an-hour, constituted the ordinary extent of his application."[98] He was in truth a dull lad, and Thackeray was probably right in his belief that "the cleverest tutors in the world could have done little probably to expand that small intellect, though they might have improved his taste and taught his perceptions some generosity."[99]

Yet those who expected the worst from the new King were pleasurably disappointed, for, though he never became a great monarch, he developed unsuspected good qualities. In earlier days his indolence had brought upon him a severe reproof from George Scott, who, when his Royal Highness excused his own want of application on the score of idleness, said, cruelly perhaps, but certainly with truth: "Sir, *yours* is not idleness; your brother Edward is *idle*, but you must not call being asleep all day being idle." On his accession to the throne, George III became suddenly industrious, at once endeavoured to understand public business, and showed himself willing to learn. Indeed, he had always been desirous to improve his mind, and it has been told how when he and Prince Edward once went by water to Woolwich he did not make a *gala* day of it, as his brother did, and as most other boys would have, "but paid a marked attention to everything useful and curious, taking a view of the several works in the dockyard, seeing the manner of forging an anchor, or making sails, etc."[100]

More remarkable than his devotion to business was the aptitude the young man, ignorant of affairs, soon showed for King-craft, and all were astonished to find that, after he had become accustomed to his position, he not only made efforts to induce ministers to carry out his views, but actually found means usually to compel them to do so. Unfortunately he started in life with the rooted idea that those who agreed with him were right, and those who differed wrong. "He will seldom do wrong, except when he mistakes wrong for right," prophesied Lord Waldegrave; "but as often as this shall happen, it will be difficult to undeceive him, because he has strong prejudices."[101] How true this was will presently appear. It was a misfortune, too, that what intelligence he possessed, not sufficient to enable him to see two sides to a question, made him suspicious of all who rose above mediocrity. Fox, father and son, he hated, and he declared once that Sheridan ought to be hanged, while he could rarely find a good word for Chatham, Burke, and the other men of commanding talent with whom perforce he was brought into contact. It was his liking for nonentities that Peter Pindar[102] pilloried, in words attributed to Sir Joseph Banks:[103]

"To circles of pure ignorance conduct me;

> I hate the company that can *instruct* me;
> I wish to imitate my King, so *nice*,
> Great prince, who ne'er was known to take advice!
> Who keeps no company (delightful plan!)
> That dares be wiser than himself, good man!"[104]

Whatever forebodings may have been entertained by those behind the scenes, George III was at his succession very popular, and whenever he showed himself in public was heartily greeted by his loyal subjects. "The new reign dates with great propriety and decency, the civilest letter to Princess Emily; the greatest kindness to the Duke; the utmost respect to the dead body," Walpole wrote. "No changes to be made but those absolutely necessary, as the household, etc.—and, what some will think the most unnecessary, in the representative of power. There is great dignity and grace in the King's manner. I don't say this like my dear Madame de Sévigné, because he was civil to *me*, but the part is well acted. The young King has all the appearance of being amiable. There is great grace to temper much dignity and good nature which breaks out on all occasions." Nicholls expressed his opinion that the monarch was "of a good person, sober, temperate, of domestic habits, addicted to no vice, swayed by no passion";[105] while Mary Lepel, Lady Hervey, was outspoken in his favour. "Every one, I think, seems to be pleased with the whole behaviour of our young King; and indeed so much unaffected good nature and propriety appears in all he does or says, that it cannot but endear him to all; but whether anything can long endear a King or an angel in this strange factious country, I can't tell. I have the best opinion imaginable of him, not from anything he does or says just now, but because I have a moral certainty that he was in his nursery the honestest, true, good-natured child that ever lived, and you know my old maxim that qualities never change; what the child was, the man most certainly is, in spite of temporary appearances."[106] Whitehead, of course, salvoed his joy in rhyme.

> "And who is he, of regal mien,
>   Reclined on Albion's golden fleece,
> Whose polished brow, and eye serene,
>   Proclaim him elder-born of peace?

[Pg 84]

> Another George! ye winds convey
>   Th' auspicious name from pole to pole:
> Thames, catch the sound and tell the subject sea
>   Beneath whose sway its waters roll,
>   The heavy monarch of the deep
> Who soothe's its murmurs with a father's care,
>   Doth now eternal Sabbath keep,
> And leaves his trident to his blooming heir,
> O, if the Muse, aright divine,
>   Fair Peace shall bless his opening reign,
> And through the splendid progress shine
>   With every art to grace her train,
> The wreaths, so late by glory won,

>   Shall weave their foliage round his throne,
>   'Till Kings abashed shall tremble to be foes,
>   And Albion's dreaded strength secure the world's repose."

Yet there were other observers who could see the reverse side of the shield. Old Samuel Johnson thought the pleasure manifested at the accession of George III, "of whom we are so much inclined to hope great things that most of them begin already to believe them," was due in great part to the fact that "we were so weary of our old King." He was, moreover, not very enthusiastic at the prospect. "The young man is hitherto blameless, but it would be unreasonable to expect much from the immaturity of juvenile years and the ignorance of princely education. He has long been in the hands of the Scots, and has already favoured them more than the English will contentedly endure. But, perhaps, he scarcely knows whom he has distinguished, or whom he has disgusted." Lord Chesterfield declared that the King, "like a new Sultan, was lugged out of the seraglio by the Princess and Lord Bute, and placed upon the throne";[107] Mr. Attorney General Pratt,[108] within four months of the accession, could "see already that this will be a weak and inglorious reign"; while Charles Townshend, asked what was the young King's character, summed it up, "He is very obstinate." [109]

CHAPTER V

"THE FAIR QUAKER"

Stolid, unimaginative, and slow of thought, that Prince of Wales, who was afterwards George III, is one of the last persons in the world to be suspected of a love intrigue. Yet, by some strange irony, he has been generally accepted as the hero of an *affaire-de-cœur* in his youthful days, and this is not the less remarkable because, so far as is known, belief has been induced only by persistent rumour. No direct evidence, personal or documentary, has ever been brought forward in support of the story; and there is no mention of it in the memoirs of George's contemporaries: even Horace Walpole, who referred to George as "chaste," never mentioned it, and it is inconceivable that that arrant scandal-monger could have been acquainted with such a tit-bit of court gossip and have refrained from retailing it. None the less there is a marked reluctance to dismiss as baseless the alleged connexion between George and Hannah Lightfoot, for, on the principle that there is no smoke without fire, it seems extremely unlikely that the story can have become so generally accepted unless it had at least some foundation of truth.

By permission of Messrs. Henry From the portrait by Sir

Graves & Co., Ltd.   *Joshua Reynolds*
MISS AXFORD
(*supposed to be a portrait of Hannah Lightfoot*)

Mr. Thoms, who many years ago made an exhaustive study of the subject[110], states that the first mention of it in print was to be found in a letter to the editor of "The Monthly Magazine, or British Register" for April, 1821, that is, after the death of George III; and this, coupled with the absence of any reference to the story in the memoirs of the day, threw very grave doubt on the authenticity of the alleged romance. Since the appearance of Mr. Thom's *brôchure*, however, this particular reason for scepticism has been removed, for earlier allusions have been discovered. "The Citizen" for Saturday, February 24, 1776, contains the following advertisement:—"*Court Fragments*. Which will be published by 'The Citizen' for the Use, Instruction and Amusement of Royal Infants and young promising Noblemen. 1. The history and adventures of Miss L-hf—t, the Fair Quaker; wherein will be faithfully portrayed some striking pictures of female constancy and princely gratitude, which terminated in the untimely death of that lady, and the sudden death of a disconsolate mother." The next recorded reference is in the "Royal Register" for 1779, when the matter is referred to as one familiar to most persons. "It is not believed even at this time, by many people who live in the world, that he [King George] had a mistress previous to his marriage. Such a circumstance was reported by many, believed by some, disputed by others, but proved by none; and with such a suitable caution was this intrigue conducted that if the body of the people called Quakers, of which this young lady in question was a member, had not divulged the fact by the public proceedings of their meeting concerning it, it would in all probability have remained a matter of doubt to this day."

Robert Huish, who wrote a life of George III, that, published in 1821, must have been in part, at least, written during the monarch's life, was also acquainted with the legend, for, though he does not mention the girl's name, he makes a very obvious allusion to Hannah Lightfoot. He states that after the Prince of Wales, at his mother's express desire, declined to entertain George II's proposal for him to marry Princess Sophia of Brunswick and stated he would wed only a Princess of the House of Saxe-Gotha, his thoughts turned to love. "The Prince, though surrounded with all the emblems of royalty, and invested with sovereign authority, was nevertheless but a man, subject to all the frailties of his nature, impelled by the powerful tide of passion," writes Huish in his grandiloquent fashion; and, after some extravagantly phrased remarks on the temptations that surround an heir-apparent, continues, "His affections became enchained; he looked no more to Saxe-Gotha nor to Brunswick for an object on which to lavish his love; he found one in the secret recesses of Hampton, whither he often repaired, concealed by the protecting shades of night, and there he experienced, what seldom falls to the lot of princes, the bliss of the purest love. The object of his affections became a mother, and strengthened the bond between them."

The reference to the affair in the letter of a correspondent "B" to "The Monthly Magazine" has, at least, the merit of being more explicit than that of the historian. "All the world is acquainted with the attachment of the late King to a beautiful Quakeress of the name of Wheeler. The lady disappeared on the royal marriage, in a way that has always been interesting, because unexplained and mysterious. I have been told she is still alive, or was lately. As connected with the life of the late sovereign, the subject is curious; and any information through your pages would doubtless be agreeable to many of your readers." It appears that the writer of this letter attributed too much knowledge to "all the world," for, as will now be shown, it is remarkable how little was known. The subject once started, however, there were plenty of people ready to carry on the discussion.

In the July number of the same periodical "A Warminster Correspondent" states that the name of the girl was not Wheeler but Hannah Lightfoot, that Hannah had lived at the corner of St. James's Market, with her mother and father, who kept a shop ("I believe a linen-draper's"), that the Prince of Wales saw her, fell in love, and persuaded Elizabeth Chudleigh, one of his mother's maids of honour,[111] to act on his behalf. "The royal lover's relations took alarm, and sent to inquire for a young man to marry her," he continues. "Isaac Axford was a shopman to Barton the grocer, on Ludgate Hill, and used to chat with her when she came to the shop to buy groceries. Perryn, of Knightsbridge, it was said, furnished a place of meeting for the royal lover. An agent of Miss Chudleigh called on Axford, and proposed that on his marrying Hannah he should have a considerable sum of money. Hannah stayed a short time with her husband, when she was taken off in a carriage, and Isaac never saw her more. Axford learned that she was gone with Miss Chudleigh. Isaac was a poorheaded fellow, or, by making a bustle about it, he might have secured to himself a good provision. He told me, when I last saw him, that he presented a petition at St. James's, which was not attended to; also that he had received some money from Perryn's assignees on account of his wife." Isaac, it seems, set up as a grocer at Warminster, his native place, but retired from business before his death, which took place about 1816 in the eighty-sixth year of his age; having long before, believing his wife to be dead, married a Miss Bartlett, of Keevil, North Wilts. "Hannah was fair and pure as far as I ever heard," the Warminster correspondent concludes, "but 'not the purest of all pures' in respect of the house of Mr. Perryn, who left her an annuity of £40 a year. She was, indeed, considered as one of the most beautiful women of her time, disposed to *en bon point*."

The editor of "The Monthly Magazine" now became interested in the matter, and himself took some trouble to elucidate the facts. "On inquiry of the Axford family, who still are respectable grocers on Ludgate Hill, we traced a son of the person alluded to in the letter, by his second wife, Miss Bartlett, and ascertained that the information of our correspondent is substantially correct. From him we learn that the lady lived six weeks with her husband, who was fondly attached to her, but one evening when he happened to be from home, a coach and four came to the door, when she was conveyed into it and carried off at a gallop, no one knew whither. It appears the husband was inconsolable at first, and at different times applied for satisfaction about his wife at Weymouth and other places, but died after sixty years in total ignorance of her fate. It has, however, been reported that she had three sons by her lover, since high in the Army; that she was buried in Islington under another name—and even that she is still living."[112]

The research of the editor of "The Monthly Magazine" bears out in the main his correspondent's statements, and if in one account it is said that Axford was shopman to Barton the grocer on Ludgate Hill, and in the other that he was the son of a grocer on Ludgate Hill, these may be reconciled by the acceptance of the theory that the man was not serving his apprenticeship in his father's business. It is far more unlikely that Hannah should go from St. James's Market to Ludgate Hill to purchase her groceries. It is agreed that Hannah stayed with her husband for a while after marriage, and it is not unnatural that the Axford family should suppress the mention of money paid to their forbear and of the circumstances that induced the payment. A more serious discrepancy, however, comes to light. "A Warminster Correspondent" remarks that Axford knew Hannah was with Miss Chudleigh; the family declares he was ignorant of what happened to her, but say at the same time he "applied about his wife at Weymouth." Why Weymouth, where George III sometimes went, if he did not know what had happened to her? Why not Barnstaple, or Leeds, or Edinburgh?

But now contradictions come fast and furious. "Isaac Axford never cohabited with his wife. She was taken away from the church door the same day they were married, and he never heard of her afterwards" states a contributor to the September number of "The Monthly Magazine"; adding that Hannah was frequently seen at the door of the St. James's Market shop by the Prince of Wales as he drove by in going to and from Parliament and that Axford (who was shopman to Bolton the grocer in Ludgate Hill) subsequently presented a petition to the King about her in the park, but obtained little address. The same writer clears Hannah's reputation so far as Perryn is concerned, by stating that they were relatives, and thus furnishing an innocent motive for the legacy.

As confusion became worse confounded, some level-headed man asked a series of questions,[113] of which the most pertinent were: "When and where did the marriage take place of Hannah Lightfoot, a Quaker, to I. Axford? Where is the evidence that she was the same Quaker who lived at the corner of St. James's Market, and was admired by Prince George?" Facts, however, were just what were not forthcoming, though "Inquirer" (who claimed to be a member of the Lightfoot family), in a letter to the October issue of the magazine actually gives a date.

"Hannah Lightfoot, when residing with her father and mother, was frequently seen by the King when he drove to and from Parliament House," "Inquirer" says. "She eloped in 1754, and was married to Isaac Axford at Keith's Chapel, which my father discovered about three weeks after, and none of her family have seen her since, though her mother had a letter or two from her—but at last died of grief. There were many fabulous stories about her, but my aunt (the mother of Hannah Lightfoot) could never trace any to be true." "Inquirer" states that "the general belief of her friends was that she was taken into keeping by Prince George directly after her marriage with Axford, but never lived with him," and adds, "I have lately seen a half-pay cavalry officer from India, who knew a gentleman of the name of Dalton, who married a daughter of Hannah Lightfoot by the King, but who is dead."[114]

So far, then, Hannah Lightfoot (or Wheeler, or, as another writer says, Whitefoot) was seen by the Prince of Wales on his visits to Parliament (or, as it is otherwise stated by one who declared that the Prince would not have passed by St. James's Market on his way to Parliament, or on his way to the Opera), who fell in love with her, and secured the aid of Miss Chudleigh to persuade her to leave her home, but his family, being alarmed, paid Isaac Axford, shopman to Barton (or Bolton) to marry her, and then she was at once (or after six weeks) taken into keeping by the Prince. This is not very plain sailing, but the incident took place more than sixty years before the discussion arose, and the discrepancies are not unnatural after that lapse of time; but at least there has been given the place and date of the marriage of Hannah with Isaac—Keith's Chapel, 1754. Alexander Keith was a clergyman who married parties daily between the hours of ten and four for the fee of one guinea, inclusive of the licence, at the Mayfair Chapel to which he gave his name. These marriages were irregular or "Fleet" marriages, and Keith's carelessness in conducting them subjected him in October, 1742, to public excommunication, when, in return, he as publicly excommunicated the bishop of the diocese, and Dr. Trebeck, the rector of the neighbouring St. George's,

Hanover Square, on being told a stop would be put to his marrying. "Then," said he, "I'll buy two or three acres of ground, and, by God, I'll *underbury* them all!" However, the Marriage Act of 1753 put a stop to his trade.

As a matter of fact, according to the Register of Marriages at St. George's Chapel, Mayfair, published in 1889 by the Harleian Society, Hannah Lightfoot married Isaac Axford, of St. Martin's, Ludgate, at Keith's Chapel on December 11, 1753. Therefore, her intrigue with George must have taken place when he was fifteen years of age!

So far as "The Monthly Magazine" is concerned the discussion ceased in 1822, but a new point was raised two years later in "An Historical Fragment relative to her late Majesty Queen Caroline," for, according to this work, Hannah Lightfoot had married not Axford, but the Prince of Wales. "The Queen (Caroline) at this time, laboured under a very curious and, to me unaccountable, species of delusion. She fancied herself in reality neither a queen nor a wife. She believed his present Majesty to have been actually married to Mrs. Fitzherbert; and she as fully believed that his late Majesty George the Third was married to Miss Hannah Lightfoot, the beautiful Quakeress, previous to his marriage with Queen Charlotte; and as that lady did not die until after the birth of the present King and his Royal Highness the Duke of York, her Majesty really considered the Duke of Clarence the true heir to the throne."

The marriage of Hannah Lightfoot and the Prince of Wales is insisted upon in the scurrilous "Authentic Records of the Court of England for the last Seventy Years" (which includes in its list of contents such items as "The Bigamy of George the Third" and "The Infamous and cold-blooded MURDERS of the Princess Charlotte, and of Caroline, Queen of England") and in "The Secret History of the Court of England." "The unhappy sovereign while Prince of Wales was in the daily habit of passing through St. James's Street and its immediate vicinity," so runs a passage in the "Secret History." "In one of his favourite rides through that part of the town he saw a very engaging young lady, who appeared by her dress to be a member of the Society of Friends. The Prince was much struck by the delicacy and lovely appearance of this female, and for several succeeding days was observed to walk out alone. At length the passion of his Royal Highness arrived at such a point that he felt his happiness depended upon receiving the lady in marriage. Every individual in his immediate circle or in the list of the Privy Council was very narrowly questioned by the Prince, though in an indirect manner, to ascertain who was most to be trusted, that he might secure, honourably, the possession of the object of his ardent wishes. His Royal Highness, at last, confided his views to his next brother, Edward, Duke of York, and another person, who were the only witnesses to the *legal* marriage of the Prince of Wales to the before-mentioned lady, Hannah Lightfoot, which took place at Curzon Street Chapel, Mayfair, in the year 1759. This marriage was productive of *issue*."

Later in the same book it is stated that George III, after his marriage with Princess Charlotte of Mecklenburg-Strelitz, reproached himself with cowardice because he had not avowed the earlier and secret union. "At this period of increased anxiety to His Majesty, Miss Lightfoot was disposed of during a temporary absence of his brother Edward, and from that time no *satisfactory* tidings ever reached those most interested in her welfare. The only information that could be obtained was that a young gentleman, named Axford, was offered a large amount, to be paid on the consummation of his marriage with Miss Lightfoot, which offer he willingly accepted. The King was greatly distressed to ascertain the fate of his much-beloved and legally-married wife, the Quakeress, and entrusted Lord Chatham to go in disguise and endeavour to trace her abode; but the search proved fruitless." The "Secret History" contains other references to this story, and it is narrated how the King, during his madness in 1765 frequently demanded the presence of "the wife of his choice," and showed the utmost disgust when the Queen was brought to him; and how, on another occasion he is declared to have implored not to be disturbed with "retrospection of past irreparable injury." Many years later, Dr. Doran gives credence to the report that when Queen Charlotte sent for her eldest son on hearing of his marriage with Mrs. Fitzherbert, he said, "My father would have been a happier man if he had remained true to his marriage with Hannah Lightfoot."

In "The Appeal for Royalty" (1858) there are given copies of two marriage certificates; the first dated Kew Chapel, April 17, 1759, signed "George P., Hannah"; the second "at this residence at Peckham," May 27, 1759, signed "George Guelph, Hannah Lightfoot;" the officiating clergyman being J. Wilmot, and the witnesses William Pitt and Anna Taylor. The same book contains also a copy of Hannah's will.

"Hampstead, July 7, 1763.

"Provided I depart this life, I recommend my two sons and my daughter to the kind protection of their Royal Father, my husband his Majesty George III, bequeathing whatever property I may die possessed of to such dear offspring of my ill-fated marriage. In case of the death of each of my children, I give and bequeath to Olive Wilmot, the daughter of my best friend, Dr. Wilmot, whatever property I am entitled to, or possessed of at the time of my death. Amen.

"(signed) HANNAH Regina.

"Witnesses   J. DUNNING.
              "WILLIAM PITT."

These documents in "The Appeal for Royalty" have, however, been proved in a court of law to be "gross and rank forgeries," and, indeed, their authenticity can never, for a moment, have been accepted. Nor do the statements in the "Historical Fragment" concerning Queen Charlotte carry conviction, even though Bradlaugh, in his "House of Hanover," remarks that Hannah Lightfoot died in the winter of 1764," and "in the early part of the year 1765, the King being then scarcely sane, a second ceremony of marriage with the Queen was then privately performed by the Rev. A. Wilmot at Kew Palace."

Still, there remains the fact that the statements in the "Authentic Records" and in "The Secret History" corroborate each other; but it would be strange if this were not so, for there is little doubt that, though the first was issued anonymously and the second bears upon the title-page Lady Anne Hamilton, the real author of both was Mrs. Olivia Serres. When it is added that in all probability Mrs. Serres also wrote the "Historical Fragment" and that her daughter, Mrs. Ryves, was responsible for "The Appeal for Royalty," it is seen that in all probability the marriage of Hannah to the heir-apparent was made (and, most likely, invented) by one person only.[115]

That George III may have married Hannah Lightfoot is not in itself unthinkable, for royalty has before and since allied itself to maids of low degree. George III's brother, Henry, Duke of Cumberland, married Mrs. Horton, while William, Duke of Gloucester, chose for his wife the Dowager Countess of Waldegrave, and even after the passing of the Royal Marriage Act the prince who was afterwards George IV went through the ceremony of marriage with a lady belonging to the Roman Catholic Church, thus defying the provisions of that Bill and of the Act of Settlement. If George III married Hannah Lightfoot, then, as there was then no Royal Marriage Act, Hannah Lightfoot was Queen of England. There is, however, no evidence to establish even a justifiable suspicion of a marriage between the Prince of Wales and Hannah Lightfoot. It is incredible that the Great Commoner should have been a witness, and it is not to be believed that in disguise he sought for the girl. Still, Pitt may not have been a witness and neither with or without disguise may he have sought for Hannah, and yet the story may not be without some foundation. It must be admitted, however, that even the many statements as to an intrigue between the couple have been based upon hearsay: no one who knew Hannah during the time it is alleged she was the Prince's mistress has spoken, and the nearest approach to direct testimony has been obtained from one who knew Axford or others who knew members of the Lightfoot or Axford families. Yet Jesse, Justin McCarthy, and other writers on George III, accept the theory of the intrigue, and without reserve, though it is in contradiction to all that is known of the young man's character at that time. Indeed, George Scott, his tutor, told Mrs. Calderwood that while the Prince of

Wales "has the greatest temptation to gallant with the ladies, who lay themselves out in the most shameful manner to draw him in," their efforts did not attract the Prince, for he realized that "if he were not what he was they would not mind him"; and, at the period of the supposed romance Scott declared that his erstwhile pupil "has no tendency to vice, and has as yet very virtuous principles;" while further contradiction of the rumour may be found in a letter written in 1731 by George III to Lord North about his son's entanglement with "Perdita" Robinson, "I am happy at being able to say that I never was personally engaged in such a transaction."

Photo by Emery Walker *From the painting by Sir Joshua Reynolds*

LADY SARAH LENNOX SACRIFICING TO THE MUSES

CHAPTER VI

LADY SARAH LENNOX AND GEORGE III[116]

It is certain that the intrigue between the Prince of Wales and Hannah Lightfoot could not have been of long duration, for even before he ascended the throne it was patent to all beholders that he was deeply infatuated with Lady Sarah Lennox, the youngest daughter of Charles, second Duke of Richmond, and a great-granddaughter of the Merry Monarch.

Lady Sarah had attracted the attention of George II one day when walking in Kensington Gardens by breaking away from her nurse or governess—she was but five years old—and addressing him without ceremony: "*Comment vous portez vous, Monsieur le roi? Vous avez une grande et belle maison ici, n'est pas?*" Her audacity pleased the sovereign, and he saw her frequently until 1751, when she was sent to Ireland to her aunt, Lady Kildare, with whom she remained until she was thirteen. Then she was placed in the care of Lady Caroline Fox[117] and not long afterwards the King, in spite of her youth, invited his favourite to court, where, however, he played and joked with her as if she was still a little child. The unexpected treatment embarrassed her; she could find nothing to say, and shyly kept her eyes on the ground, whereupon the King turned from her, saying, "Pooh! she's quite stupid." The young Prince of Wales was "struck with admiration and pity" at this sight of beauty in distress, and then and there, we are told, fell in love—thus showing an appreciation of good looks that was not common with the Georges.

Lady Sarah, who was not fifteen when she went to Court in November, 1759, was indeed, alike according to her portraits and to all contemporary chroniclers, a most lovely girl. "Her beauty is not easily described otherwise than by saying she had the finest complexion, most beautiful hair, and prettiest person that ever was seen, with a sprightly and fine air, a pretty mouth, and remarkably fine teeth, and excess of bloom in her cheeks, little eyes," said her uncle, Henry Fox. "This is not describing her, for her great beauty was a peculiarity of countenance that made her at the same time different from and prettier than any other girl I ever saw."[118] Walpole is quite as enthusiastic about her charms in a letter to George Montagu, written in January, 1761. "There was a play at Holland House, acted by children; not all children, for Lady Sarah Lennox and Lady Susan Strangways played the women. It was 'Jane Shore.' Charles Fox was Hastings. The two girls were delightful and acted with so much nature, that they appeared the very things they represented. Lady Sarah was more beautiful than you can conceive; her very awkwardness gave an air of truth to the sham of the part, and the antiquity of the time, kept up by the dress, which was taken out of Montfaucon. Lady Susan was dressed from Jane Seymour. I was more struck with the last scene between the two women than ever I was when I have seen it on the stage. When Lady Sarah was in white, with her hair about her ears, and on the ground, no Magdalen of Correggio was half so lovely and expressive."

After the death of his grandfather, George III made no effort to hide the state of his feelings. Of course, the Princess Dowager came to know of her son's attachment to Lady Sarah, and she and Lord Bute were aghast at the notion of the King marrying the girl, for such an alliance would be even more fatal to their influence on the young monarch than the frustrated union with a princess of the House of Brunswick, since in this case they would have to contend, not only against the power of a fascinating bride, but also against the intrigues of such an astute politician as Henry Fox, who had everything to gain by excluding them from the King's councils. On the other hand, Fox, his hand strengthened by the fact that the laws of England do not forbid the sovereign to mate with a subject, did all he could to promote the union that must benefit him. So while the principals in that love affair played their parts, behind them was a bitter fight that was not the less severe because it could not come to open warfare.

Fox was careful that his niece, Lady Sarah, should stay at Holland House so long as the King was in town, but discreetly himself went from time to time to his house at Kingsgate in the Isle of Thanet, very wisely realizing that the strongest card in his hand was the charm of the young girl. "Though Fox went himself to bathe in the sea, and possibly even to disguise his intrigues," Walpole wrote in 1761, "he left Lady Sarah at Holland House, where she appeared in a field close to the great road (where the King passed on horseback) in a fancy habit making hay."

The course of true love ran smoothly enough for a while. The King was young and handsome, and Lady Sarah, not averse to be a queen, received his overtures graciously. So far, indeed, had the affair progressed early in 1761, that the King confided his passion to Lady Sarah's friend, Lady Susan Fox Strangways,[119] with whom he had the following guarded conversation:

"You are going into Somersetshire; when do you return?"

"Not before winter, sir, or I don't know how soon in winter."

"Is there nothing will bring you back to town before winter?"

"I don't know of anything."

"Would you not like to see a Coronation?"

"Yes, sir. I hope I should come to see that."

"I hear it's very popular my having put it off.... Won't it be a much finer sight when there is a Queen?"

"To be sure, sir."

"I have had a great many applications from abroad, but I don't like them. I have had none at home: I should like that better.... What do you think of your friend? You know who I mean; don't you think her fittest?"

"Think, sir?"

"I think none so fit."[120]

According to Thomas Pitt, Lady Susan was much embarrassed when the King said, "I have had no applications at home: I should like that better," as, for an instant, she thought he meant her, but her agitation was dissipated when he continued, "I mean your friend, Lady Sarah Lennox. Tell her so, and let me have her answer the next Drawing-room day."[121] Fox, however, makes no allusion to this, and merely records that the King crossed over to Lady Sarah, and told her to ask her friend what he had been saying.

A week later the King asked Lady Sarah if she had heard what he had said, and upon her replying in the affirmative, put the question, "Do you approve?" to which he received as answer only a cross look, whereupon, in high dudgeon, he left the room. This brusque repulse is explained by the fact that Lady Sarah was piqued by her lover, Lord Newbattle,[122] and sought solace by avenging his offence upon her royal suitor. Fox remarked the coolness of the King, and commented, "He has undoubtedly heard of Lord Newbattle and more than is true;" but soon the sovereign's love conquered his dignity, and perhaps a reconciliation was hastened by the news of an accident in the hunting field to Lady Sarah. Lord Newbattle when told she had fractured a leg had said, "It will do no great harm, for her legs were ugly enough before," and this statement, repeated to Lady Sarah, cured her of her attachment to the speaker, and made her more ready, on her recovery, to accede to the King's request to reconsider his proposal.

But this marriage was not to be. "They talk very strongly of a white Princess of Brunswick about fifteen, to be our new Queen, and so strongly that one can hardly help believing it, though with no good and particular authority," Fox wrote on April 7, 1761; though a week later he recorded: "On Sunday I heard from good authority that the report of his Majesty's intended marriage with a Princess of Brunswick was entirely without foundation, and that he was totally free and unengaged." That Fox was incredulous as to the King's marriage with a princess was not unnatural, considering the monarch's conduct. "At the court ball on his Majesty's birthday, June 4, 1761, Lady Sarah's place was, of course, at the head of the dancers' bench, nearest his seat: the royal chair, heavy as it was, was moved nearer and nearer to the left, and he edged further and further the same way, and the conversation went on till all dancing was over and everybody sat in suspense; and it approached one in the morning ere he recollected himself and rose to dismiss the assembly."[123] On June 18 the King said to Lady Sarah: "For God's sake remember what I said to Lady Susan before you went to the country, and believe that I have the strongest attachment." Yet within a fortnight of explicit declaration, which was well received by the girl, a Council was summoned for July 8, though even on the 6th Fox could obtain no hint from Lord Bute as to the business to be transacted. At the meeting of the Council the King announced his forthcoming marriage with Princess Charlotte of Mecklenburg-Strelitz!

Lady Susan Fox Strangways was more aggrieved than the person chiefly concerned, for, as she remarked humorously, "I almost thought myself Prime Minister"; but Fox was furious, as much at the deception as at the disappointment. "My mother (Lady Sarah) would probably have been vexed," said Henry Napier, "but her favourite squirrel happened to die at the same time, and his loss was more felt than that of a crown."[124] Lady Sarah was not in love with the King, and the shock fell not on her heart but on her vanity. "I did not cry, I assure you, which I believe you will, as I know you were set upon it that I was," she wrote on July 7, 1761, to Lady Susan. "The thing I am most angry at is looking so like a fool, as I shall for having gone so often for nothing, but I don't much care; if he was to change his mind again (which can't be though), and not give me a *very* good reason for his conduct, I would not have him, for if he is so weak as to be governed by everybody, I shall have but a bad time of it." She certainly had reason to complain of the King's conduct, and, after referring to his "mighty kind speeches and looks," this she did to the same correspondent. "Even last Thursday, the day after the orders [for the Council] were come out," she wrote, "the hypocrite had the face to come up and speak to me with all the good humour in the world, and seemed to want to speak to me but was afraid.... He must have sent to this woman [Princess Charlotte] before you went out of town, then what business had he to begin again? In short, his behaviour is that of a man who has neither sense, good nature, nor honesty."[125]

The King's conduct at this juncture has never been satisfactorily explained. "It is well known," Wraxall wrote, "that before his marriage the King distinguished by his partiality Lady Sarah Lennox, then one of the most beautiful young women of high rank in the kingdom. Edward IV, or Henry VIII, in his situation, would have married and placed her on the throne.

Charles II, more licentious, would have endeavoured to seduce her. But the King, though he admired her, neither desired to make her his wife nor his mistress, subdued his passion by the strength of his reason, his principles, and his sense of public duty."[126]

This statement is certainly inaccurate, at least in so far as the remark that the King did not desire to make Lady Sarah his wife, for all the evidence—which was not available in Wraxall's day—tends to prove that for a while this was his wish. There is more truth in the supposition that his sense of public duty intervened in favour of a lady of royal birth, though this furnishes no reason for keeping his intention secret from Lady Sarah. Doubtless he was persuaded by his mother and Lord Bute that it was his duty to espouse a princess, and, once convinced of this, he sighed and sighed, and rode away.

Fox knew he was beaten, but he showed a philosophic calm. "Well, Sal," he said to his niece, "you are the first virgin in England, and you shall take your place in spite of them all as chief bridesmaid, and the King shall behold your pretty face and repent." But the twain met again so early as July 16 when Lady Sarah went to Court. "I went this morning for the first time," she wrote to her friend. "He looked frightened when he saw me, but notwithstanding came up with what countenance I don't know for I was not so gracious as ever to look at him: when he spoke our conversation was short. Here it is. 'I see riding is begun again, it's glorious weather for it now.' Answer. 'Yes, it is very fine,'—and add to that a very cross and angry look of my side and his turning away immediately, and you know the whole."[127]

Lady Sarah, as her uncle had promised, was duly appointed chief bridesmaid, and perhaps she felt herself avenged, for, according to Princess Amelia, "Upon my word my nephew has most wonderful assurance; during the ceremony he never took his eyes from Lady Sarah, or cast them once upon his bride."[128] It was remarked that the King moved uneasily when the Archbishop of Canterbury read the lines of the marriage service: "And as Thou didst send Thy blessing upon Abraham and Sarah to their great comfort, so vouchsafe to send Thy blessing upon these Thy servants"; but it has not been recorded how the King felt when, at the Drawing-room held on the next day, the old Earl of Westmoreland mistook Lady Sarah for the Queen and was only prevented just in time from kneeling and kissing her hand.[129]

That the King never forgot Lady Sarah Lennox is certain. When at the theatre he saw Mrs. Pope, who much resembled Lady Sarah, he fell into a reverie, and, forgetful of the Queen and other persons in his box, mused: "She is like Lady Sarah still"; while Princess Elizabeth told Lady Louisa Stuart, "Do you know papa says she (Princess Mary) will be like Lady Sarah Bunbury, who was the prettiest woman he ever saw in his life." Lady Sarah was well content with her lot, and, as is well known, made in 1762 "a match of her own choice" with the sporting baronet, Sir Thomas Charles Bunbury, and, when this union was dissolved in 1781, married the Hon. George Napier, [130] and became the mother of eight children, two of whom, William and Charles, attained distinction as, respectively, the historian of the Peninsular War and the conqueror of Scinde.[131] But we have no concern here with the later years of Lady Sarah, save to remark that she never regretted the loss of the brilliant position to which she so nearly attained. "I declare that I have for years reverenced the Queen's name, and admired the judgment of Providence in placing so exalted a character in a station where my miserable one would have been a disgrace!" she wrote in 1789 to Lady Susan O'Brien. "And now I still affirm the judgment of Providence is always right, but I see she was chosen to punish the poor King's faults by her ambitions and conduct instead of *me* by my faults, and I *still* rejoice I was never Queen, and so I shall to my life's end; for, at the various events in it, I have regularly catechised myself upon that very point, and I always preferred my own situation, sometimes happy, sometimes miserable, to what it would have been had that event ever taken place." One other quotation from a letter from Lady Sarah to the same correspondent may perhaps be allowed. "I am one who will keep the King's marriage-day with unfeigned joy and gratitude to Heaven that I am not in her Majesty's place! It was the happiest day for me, in as much [as] I like to attend my dear sick husband better than a King. I like my sons better than I like the royal sons, thinking them better animals, and more likely to give me comfort in my old age; and I like better to be a subject, than subject to the terrors of royalty in these days of trouble. It's pleasant to have lived to be satisfied of the great advantages of a lot which in those days I might have deemed unlucky. Ideas of fifteen and sixty one cannot well assimilate; but mine began at fourteen, for if you remember I was not near fifteen when my poor head began to be turned by adulation, in consequence of my supposed favour. In the year 1759, on the late Princess of Wales's birthday, November 30, I ought to have been in my nursery, and I shall ever think it was unfair to bring me into the world while a child. *Au reste*, I am delighted to hear the King is so well, for I am excessively partial to him. I always consider him as an old friend that has been in the wrong; but does one love one's friend less for being in the wrong even towards oneself? I don't, and I would not value the friendship of those who measure friendship by my deservings. God help me if all my friends thought thus."[132]

CHAPTER VII

THE ROYAL MARRIAGE

The rumour that the King would espouse a Princess of Brunswick had arisen from a proposal to that effect made by the Princess Dowager, but for many reasons this suggestion was not acted upon. Subsequently a princess of the house of Hesse was thought of, but her levity of conduct was such that, when it came to the point, it was found that "nobody would take it upon them to recommend her." Eventually Lord Bute instructed a Colonel Graeme or Graham to visit the German courts to find a princess who should be "perfect in her form, of pure blood and healthy constitution, possessed of elegant accomplishments, particularly music, to which the King was much attached, and of a mild and obliging disposition." The appointment of Graeme for this responsible errand caused much surprise, for the selected envoy had been notorious as a Jacobite; which provoked Hume to the remark that Graeme had exchanged the dangerous office of making a king for the more lucrative one of making a king's marriage. However, the envoy was conscientious, and "in the character of a private gentleman, played lotto with the ladies of one court, and drank the aperient waters with the antiquated dames of another, merely to hear the tittle-tattle of the day, respecting the positive or negative virtues, the absence or excellence of personal charms, which at that time distinguished the marriageable princesses of the numerous royal, ducal, or princely families of Protestant Germany."[133] Graeme carried out his task to the best of his ability. He had been commanded to seek a peerless Dulcinda: he found Princess Charlotte of Mecklenburg-Strelitz,[134] who subsequently rewarded him for his share in her promotion by the bestowal of one of the richest places in the gift of the Queen of England, the Mastership of St. Catherine's Hospital.

From a drawing by T. McArdell
QUEEN CHARLOTTE

There is, however, another account of the selection of Princess Charlotte as consort of George III. The King of Prussia's army had devastated the Duchy of Mecklenburg-Strelitz, and the young Princess protested in a letter to the monarch....

"May it please your Majesty, I am at a loss whether I should congratulate or condole with you on your late victory over Marshall Daun, November 3, 1760 since the same success which has covered you with laurels, has overspread the country of Mecklenburg with desolation. I know, Sire, that it seems unbecoming my sex, in this age of vicious refinement, to feel for one's country, to lament the horrors of war, or wish for the return of peace. I know you may think it more properly my province to study the arts of pleasing, or to inspect subjects of a more domestic nature; but, however unbecoming it may be in me, I cannot resist the desire of interceding for this unhappy people. It was but a very few years ago that this territory wore the most pleasing appearance; the country was cultivated, the peasants looked cheerful, and the towns abounded with riches and festivity. What an alteration at present from such a charming scene! I am not expert at description, nor can my fancy add any horrors to the picture; but surely even conquerors would weep at the hideous prospects now before me. The whole country, my dear country, lies one frightful waste, presenting only objects to excite terror, pity, and despair. The business of the husbandman and shepherd are discontinued. The husbandman and the shepherd are become soldiers themselves, and help to ravage the soil they formerly cultivated. The towns are inhabited only by old men, old women, and children; perhaps here and there a warrior, by wounds or loss of limbs, rendered unfit for service, left at his door; his little children hang round him, ask an history of every wound, and grow themselves soldiers, before they find strength for the field. But this were nothing, did we not feel the alternate insolence of either army as it happens to advance or retreat, in pursuing the operations of the campaign. It is impossible to express the confusion, even those who call themselves our friends create; even those from whom we might expect redress oppress with new calamities. From your justice, therefore, it is we hope relief. To you even women and children may complain, whose humanity stoops to the meanest petition, and whose power is capable of repressing the greatest injustice."

A copy of this document, so the story goes, found its way, either by accident or design, to George III, who, not pausing to consider that it was unlikely to have been composed by a sixteen-year-old princess, exclaimed to Lord Hertford: "This is the lady whom I shall select for my consort—here are lasting beauties—the man who has any mind may feast and not be satisfied. If the disposition of the Princess but equals her refined sense, I shall be the happiest man, as I hope, with my people's concurrence, to be the greatest monarch in Europe." If in a wife George desired such qualities as a knowledge of the elements of Lutheran divinity, natural history, and mineralogy, with some French, a trifle of Italian, and a style of drawing that even a courtier could describe only as "above that of the ordinary amateur," they were, for the asking, to be had in this Princess. Apparently these accomplishments sufficed, for *pourparlers* were exchanged, and the King's intention to marry Princess Charlotte was on July 8, 1761, notified by himself to the Privy Council.

"Having nothing so much at heart as to procure the welfare and happiness of my people, and to render the same stable and permanent to posterity," he said, "I have, ever since my accession to the throne, turned my thoughts towards the choice of a Princess for my consort; and I now, with great satisfaction acquaint you, that after the fullest information and maturest deliberation, I am come to a resolution to demand in marriage the Princess Charlotte of Mecklenburg-Strelitz, a princess distinguished by every eminent virtue and amiable endowment, whose illustrious line has constantly shown the firmest zeal for the Protestant religion, and a particular attachment to my family. I have judged proper to communicate to you these my intentions, in order that you may be fully apprised of a matter so highly important to me and to my kingdom, and which I persuade myself will be most acceptable to all my loving subjects."

To this meeting of the Privy Council was summoned Lord Harcourt, who, after the King's speech, was to his great surprise informed by Lord Bute that he had been appointed Master of the Horse, and was to go to Strelitz to make formal application for the hand of the Princess. "After what happened to me some years ago, it was beneath me to become a solicitor for favours," he said. "This honour I expected about as much as I did the bishopric of London, then vacant." He accepted the mission, and on August 8 set sail for Strelitz—"if he can find it," Walpole said satirically, in allusion to the size of the Duchy, the dimensions of which were one hundred and twenty miles long by thirty miles broad.

"They say the little Princess who had written the fine letter about the horrors of war—a beautiful letter without a single blot, for which she was to be rewarded, like the heroine of the old spelling book story—was at play one day with some of her young companions in the gardens of Strelitz, and that the young lady's conversation was, strange to say, about husbands," Thackeray has written. "'Who will take such a poor little princess as me?' Charlotte said to her friend, Ida von Bülow, and at that very moment the postman's horn sounded, and Ida said, 'Princess! there is the sweetheart.' As she said, so it actually turned out. The postman brought letters from the splendid young King of all England, who said, 'Princess! because you have written such a beautiful letter, which does credit to your head and heart, come and be Queen of Great Britain, France, and Ireland, and the true wife of your most obedient servant, George.' So she jumped for joy; and went upstairs and packed all her little trunks; and set off straightway for her kingdom in a beautiful yacht, with a harpsichord on board for her to play upon, and around her a beautiful fleet, all covered with flags and streamers."[135]

This playful account is not, perhaps, historically correct, but, if the story is to be believed, it conveys the true spirit of the offer and its acceptance. The Princess was just seventeen years of age, and had led the quietest life imaginable, studying under Madame de Grabow, the "German Sappho," cultivating medicinal herbs and fruit for the poor, and employing her leisure with embroidery and needlework. Six days a week she had worn the simplest attire; on the seventh only, when she attended church in state, had been granted the privilege of full dress and the delight of a drive in a coach and six. Indeed, she had never dined at the ducal table until, on the arrival of Lord Harcourt, her brother Adolphus Frederick, the reigning Duke, told her she was expected to be present. "Mind what you say," he added, and "don't behave like a child"; and of course the warning produced a fit of shyness, the discomfort of which more than counterbalanced the pleasure of her first dinner party. Later in the evening, or (some authorities say) the next morning, the Duke, again cautioning her, "*Allons, ne faites pas l'enfant, tu vas être reine d'Angleterre*," led her into a drawing-room, where, after Lord Harcourt had presented some jewels from his master, the marriage ceremony was performed, with Drummond, the resident English minister at the ducal court, as the King's proxy.[136]

The treaty of marriage was signed on August 15, 1761, and although, suddenly nervous at the prospective plunge into the unknown world, the new Queen would willingly have postponed her departure for a few days longer, yet, as the coronation of her husband and herself was already fixed for September 22, she was compelled to leave Strelitz two days after the ceremony. At Stade she was met by the Duchess of Hamilton and the Duchess of Ancaster, who had come to escort the bride to her adopted country. "I hope friendship may take the place of ceremony in our relations," she greeted them, having apparently at once caught the tone of regal graciousness; and she completed the conquest of the noble dames when, after gazing at them, she said wonderingly and a little fearful: "Are all English women as beautiful as you?" Queen Charlotte was very humble in those early days, and her childish delight in the salutes with which cannons and bells greeted her was tempered with meek astonishment: "Am I worthy of all these honours?"

The royal party embarked at Cuxhaven on August 22, but did not reach Harwich until Sunday, September 6. The delay, which was occasioned by exceptionally rough weather, caused some anxiety as to the safety of the Queen, especially in London, where the news of her arrival was not known until Monday. "Last night at ten o'clock it was neither certain where she landed, nor when she would be in town," Horace Walpole wrote on Tuesday, September 8, "I forgive history for knowing nothing when so public an event as the arrival of a new queen is a mystery even at this very moment at St. James's. The messenger that brought the letter yesterday morning said she *arrived* at half-an-hour after four at Harwich; this was immediately translated into *landing*, and notified in these words to the ministers. Six hours afterwards it proved no such thing, and, that she was only in Harwich Road; and they recollected that half-an-hour after four happens twice in twenty-four hours, and the letter did not specify which of the twices it was. Well, the bridesmaids whipt on their virginity; the New Road and the Parks were thronged; the guns were choking with impatience to go off; and Sir James Lowther, who was to pledge his Majesty, was actually married to Lady Mary Stuart. Five, six, seven, eight o'clock came, and no queen."

The Queen had remained on board until three o'clock on Monday afternoon, so as to allow time for the preparations incidental to her reception. She then drove to Colchester, which was reached at five o'clock, and from there went on to Witham, where she stayed overnight at Lord Abercorn's.[137] Leaving Witham early in the morning, the Queen arrived at noon at Romford, where she was met by the King's coaches and servants. She entered one of the royal carriages, dressed in "a fly-cap with rich lace lappets, a stomacher ornamented with diamonds, and a gold brocade suit of clothes with a white ground." Her companions desired her to curl her *toupée* but this she declined to do on the ground that it looked as well as that of any of the ladies sent to fetch her, adding that if the King wished her to wear a periwig she would do so, but otherwise would remain as she was.

From Romford the Queen and her attendants, watched by immense crowds, proceeded to "Stratford-le-bow and Mile-end turnpike, where they turned up Dog-row, and prosecuted their journey to Hackney turnpike, then by Shoreditch Church, and up Old Street to the City-road, across Islington, along the New-road into Hyde Park, down Constitutional-hill into St. James's Park." At the sight of the Palace, the Queen turned pale, and, noticing that the Duchess of Hamilton smiled, "My dear Duchess," she said, "you may laugh; you have been married twice, but it is no joke to me." At twenty minutes past three in the afternoon she arrived at St. James's, and Walpole remarked that the "noise of the coaches, chaises, horsemen, mob, that have been to see her pass through the parks is so prodigious that I cannot distinguish the guns."

The King received his bride at the entrance to the palace, and, though he had chosen her for her "lasting beauties", was so surprised by the homeliness of her features that, says Galt, "an involuntary expression of the King's countenance revealed what was passing within." Lady Anne Hamilton goes so far as to say that, "At the first sight of the German Princess, the King actually shrank from her gaze, for her countenance was of that cast that too plainly told of the nature of the spirit working within,"[138] but this is almost certainly exaggeration, and may be dismissed with the following statement by the same author: "In the meantime the Earl of Abercorn informed the Princess of the previous marriage of the King and of the existence of his Majesty's wife; and Lord Harcourt advised the Princess to well inform herself of the policy of the kingdom, as a measure for preventing much future disturbance in the country, as well as securing an uninterrupted possession of the throne to her issue. Presuming therefore that the German Princess had hitherto been an open and ingenuous character, such expositions, intimations, and dark mysteries, were ill-calculated to nourish honourable feelings, but would rather operate as a check to their further existence. To the public eye the newly married pair were contented with each other; alas! it was because each feared an exposure to the nation. The King reproached himself that he had not fearlessly avowed the only wife of his affections; the Queen because she feared an explanation that the King was guilty of bigamy, and thereby her claim, as also that of her progeny (if she should have any), would be known to be illegitimate. It appears as if the result of those reflections formed a basis for the misery of millions, and added to that number millions yet unborn."[139]

Lord Harcourt wrote from Strelitz of the bride as "no regular beauty", but credited her with a charming complexion, very pretty eyes, and a good figure, summing her up as a very fine girl, and Mrs. Papendiek, who came over with her, has placed on record a not dissimilar picture, "She was certainly not a beauty, but her countenance was expressive and intelligent. She was not tall, but of a slight, rather pretty figure; her eyes bright and sparkling with good humour and vivacity, her mouth large, but filled with white and even teeth, and her hair really beautiful." Walpole has said that within half-an-hour of her arrival in the metropolis one heard of nothing but proclamations of her beauty, but his first description of her was not flattering, and his second denies her all claim to good looks. "Her person was small and very lean, not well made; her face pale and homely, her nose somewhat flat and mouth very large. Her hair, however, was of a fine brown, and her countenance pleasing," he wrote on her arrival; but later remarked: "She had always been, if not ugly, at least ordinary, but in her later years her want of personal charms became, of course, less observable, and it used to be said that she was grown better-looking. I said one day something to this effect to Colonel Desbrowe, her Chamberlain. 'Yes,' he replied, 'I do think the *bloom* of her ugliness is going off!'"

Immediately upon her arrival the King introduced to his bride the members of his family, and soon after the royal party sat down to dinner. Later the bridesmaids[140] and the Court were introduced, and in such numbers that she exclaimed as the long procession passed before her, "*Mon Dieu, il y en a tout, il y en a tout.*" She bore herself with dignity, but was civil and good-humoured, showed pleasure when she was told she should kiss the peeresses, and betrayed a pretty reluctance to give her hand to be kissed by the humbler folk. At ten o'clock all repaired to the chapel where the marriage ceremony was repeated. The Queen was, of course, in bridal costume, and Walpole thought she looked very sensible, cheerful, and remarkably genteel. "Her tiara of diamonds was very pretty, her stomacher was sumptuous," he commented: "her violet-velvet mantle so heavy that the spectators know as much of her upper half as the King himself." This was a trying ordeal after a long journey, but the Queen forgot or disguised her fatigue, and when the party returned to the drawing-room, was quite cheerful, played the spinet and sang while the company was waiting for supper, talked French with some guests and German with her attentive husband. "It does not promise," said Walpole, "as if they would be the two most unhappy people in England."

CHAPTER VIII

THE RISE AND FALL OF THE "FAVOURITE"

The great question that agitated English political society at the accession of George III was, as a lady summed it up in a *bon-mot*, "whether the new King would burn in his chamber *Scotch* coal, *Newcastle* coal, or *Pitt* coal." The curious were not long kept in a state of suspense, for George showed at once that he was determined so far as possible to be independent of ministers not of his own choosing; and when, after his arrival in London, Pitt waited on him and presented a paper on which were written a few sentences that the Great Commoner thought the monarch should deliver at his first Council, the King, after thanking Pitt for his consideration, said he had already prepared his speech for that occasion.[141] This, as a matter of fact, he had done in conjunction with Lord Bute, and at the meeting of the Council, although at first somewhat embarrassed, he soon recovered his self-possession, and delivered himself of the address.

From an engraving after the painting by Allan Ramsay
JOHN, EARL OF BUTE

"The just concern which I have felt in my own breast on the sudden death of the late King, my royal grandfather, makes me not doubt, but that all have been deeply affected with so severe a loss. The present critical and difficult conjuncture has made this loss the more sensible, as he was the great support of that system by which alone the liberties of Europe, and the weight and influence of these kingdoms can be preserved, and give life to measures conducive to those important ends.

"I need not tell you the addition of weight which immediately falls upon me, in being called to the government of this free and powerful country at such a time, and under such circumstances. My consolation is in the uprightness of my own intentions, your faithful and united assistance, and the blessing of Heaven upon our joint endeavours, which I devoutly implore.

"Born and educated in this country, I glory in the name of Briton; and the peculiar happiness of my life will ever consist in promoting the welfare of a people whose loyalty and warm affection to me I consider as the greatest and most permanent security of my throne, and I doubt not but this steadiness in those principles will equal the firmness of my invariable resolution to adhere to, and strengthen this excellent constitution in church and state, and to maintain the toleration inviolable. The civil and religious rights of my loving subjects are equally dear to me with the most valuable prerogatives of my crown; and as the surest foundation of the whole, and the best means to draw down the divine favour on my reign, it is my fixed purpose to countenance and encourage the practice of true religion and virtue."[142]

The King's speech was well received throughout the country, although there were many who agreed with ex-Lord Chancellor Hardwicke that the since historic sentence, "Born and educated in this country, I glory in the name of Briton," was, if not an insult, at least discourteous to his last two predecessors, and the annoyance felt by some was not allayed when it became known that Bute, so as to include Scotland, had altered the "Englishman" of the first draft to "Briton" in the revised copy. To this nine years later, Junius made reference in his address to the King. "When you affectedly renounced the name of Englishman, believe me, Sir, you were persuaded to pay a very ill-judged compliment to one part of your subjects at the expense of another. While the natives of Scotland are not in actual rebellion, they are undoubtedly entitled to protection, nor do I mean to condemn the policy of giving some encouragement to the novelty of their affections for the house of Hanover. I am ready to hope for everything from their new-born zeal, and from the future steadiness of their allegiance. But hitherto they have no claim on your favour. To honour them with a determined predilection and confidence, in exclusion of your English subjects who placed your family, and, in spite of treachery and rebellion have supported it, upon the throne, is a mistake too gross even for the unsuspecting generosity of youth. In your error we see a capital violation of the most obvious rules of policy and prudence. We trace it, however, to an original bias in your education, and are ready to allow for your inexperience."

On the whole, however, the nation extended a hearty welcome to the young King and on his accession he was undoubtedly popular. At least, English was his native tongue, and this was the more agreeable because George II had spoken it with a very broad German accent, Frederick, Prince of Wales, on his arrival in England, knew but a few words of the language, and George I had not understood it at all. "My father 'brushed up his old Latin!' to use a phrase of Queen Elizabeth, in order to converse with the first Hanoverian sovereign," Horace Walpole has told us, "and ruled both kings in spite of their mistresses." Now, for the first time for six and forty years, England boasted a sovereign whose interests were not centred in Hanover, a young man, not a middle-aged reprobate surrounded with women of sullied reputations: further, the dynasty was more firmly established, and the Jacobite faction had dwindled in power from a serious menace to an empty threat. George I had been confronted with the Old Pretender, his successor had had to contend against the Young Pretender; but George III, who had nothing to fear from the Stuarts and their adherents, could increase his popularity by showing some favour to the Tories, who during the previous reigns, owing to the suspicions that they were attached to the Stuart interest, had been tabooed.

So little fear, indeed, had the reigning dynasty for the representative of that which preceded it, that though it was known Charles Edward was in London at the time of the coronation, the government made no attempt to secure his person. It is even recorded how that Prince, in answer to an inquiry how he dared venture to show himself in London, stated that he was very safe; and, indeed, this was the case, for his day had passed, the Hanoverian dynasty had firmly established itself, and the once magic name of Stuart now made no impression upon the nation. "Let sleeping dogs lie," was in this case apparently the rule by which the King and his advisers guided their conduct.
[143]

One of the first official acts of the King was to give his assent in person to an act imposing an additional duty on heavy ales and beer, but what anger this Bill evoked was directed against Bute, while the chorus of praise that greeted the King's next move was given to him alone, though it also was inspired by the favourite. After the Revolution, judges held their offices for the reign of the sovereign who appointed them, but at Bute's instigation a bill was introduced to secure their posts to them for life. This was regarded as a most gracious and constitutional measure, though according to Nicholls it was nothing of the sort. "The courtiers of George III have trumpeted this conduct as a singular mark of George III's disposition to diminish his power; but in fact George III increased his power by this measure: having no dislike to those whom he found in office, he had renewed their commissions. By the statute which he thus procured to be enacted, he rendered those judges whom he might appoint, irremovable by his successor; and thus, instead of diminishing his power he increased it."[144] Indeed, even as regards the graciousness of the act, a different complexion is placed upon it by the same authority, who said it was devised "by those who had most influence over the King" and desired to throw reproach on George II, who on his accession had not granted commissions to those judges who had offended him during his father's lifetime when he was in opposition.[145] Johnson thought it a most impolitic measure. "There is no reason," he said, "why a judge should hold his office for life more than any other person in public trust. A judge may be partial otherwise than to the Crown: we have seen judges partial to the populace. A judge may be corrupt, and yet there may be no legal evidence against him. A judge may become froward in age. A judge may grow unfit for his office in many ways. It was desirable that there should be a possibility of being delivered from him by a new king."[146] As a matter of fact, there is no doubt that the measure was devised for popularity, and in this it certainly succeeded.

The favour the King thus won in the eyes of his subjects was later increased by his surrendering, on Bute's advice, £700,000, the money from the prizes taken before the declaration of war, which, by the Peace of Paris, became the King's property; £200,000, the value of lands in the ceded islands; and by his acceptance of the fixed income of £800,000, to be paid out of the aggregate fund in lieu of the uncertain funds which then made up the Civil List.[147] Yet another thing contributed to the King's popularity, for, when, as the law then stood, Parliament dissolved six months after the royal demise, it became known that George III had instructed his ministry that no money should be spent in endeavours to secure the election of members favourable to the Court, saying "I will be tried by my country"—a sentence that was commemorated by an obscure rhymester.

> "Tried by your country! To your people's love,
>   Amiable prince, so soon appeal;
> Stay till the tender sentiments improve,
>   Ripening to gratitude from zeal.
> Years hence (yet, ah! too soon) shall Britain see
>   The trial of thy virtue past;
> Who could believe that your first wish would be
>   What all believe will be your last."[148]

A rift in the lute showed itself very soon, for almost immediately after the accession of George III, the ascendancy of Lord Bute was displayed in so many ways that it became obvious to all observers. There was some surprise when the name of the Duke of Cumberland was struck out of the liturgy, and a great deal of indignation when the favourite was made Ranger of Richmond Park in the place of Princess Amelia, who, Huish says, "was literally turned out;" but the indignation of the latter was certainly misplaced, for the Princess resigned the post as the result of a quarrel about a right of way with the townsfolk of Richmond. From the beginning of the new reign the City of London was suspicious of Lord Bute, and that powerful corporation was at no pains to disguise its feelings. "The City have a mind to be out of humour; a paper has been fixed in the Royal Exchange with these words—'No Government! No Scotch Minister! No Lord George Sackville'[149]—two hints totally unfounded, and the other scarce true. No petticoat ever governed less; it is left at Leicester House—for the King himself, he seems all good nature, and wishing to satisfy everybody; all his speeches are obliging. I saw him on the throne, where he's all graceful and genteel; sits with dignity, and reads his answers to addresses well."[150] So Horace Walpole wrote early in November, 1760; but it must be admitted that that usually keen observer did not display his usual prescience, for the "Scotch Minister" might have been sighted on the political horizon.

Indeed, almost at once negotiations were set on foot to place Bute at the head of affairs. "Lord Bute came to me by appointment, and stayed a great while," Dodington records so early in the new reign as November 29, 1760. "I pressed him much to take the Secretary's office, and provide otherwise for Lord Holdernesse; he hesitated for some time, and then said, if that was the only difficulty, it would be easily removed, for Lord Holdernesse was ready at his desire to quarrel with his fellow-ministers (on account of the slights and ill-usage which he had daily experienced), and go to the King, and throw up in seeming anger, and then he (Bute) might come in without seeming to displace anybody."[151] Bute required little persuasion to accept office, for his desire was to displace the Prime Minister and reign in his stead, and his object was so little disguised that when some time before he had been congratulated upon his appointment as Groom of the Stole to the then Prince of Wales, he had replied, he could feel no pleasure while the Duke of Newcastle was

Minister.

The King threw the full weight of his influence into the scale in Bute's favour, and at the end of January, 1761, the Duke of Newcastle told the Marquis of Rockingham, "We have received a message from the King, of great importance; he wishes that the Earl of Holdernesse may resign the place of Secretary of State for the Northern Department, and receive in lieu of it the Wardenship of the Cinque Ports, and that the Earl of Bute may be appointed Secretary of State for the Northern Department, in place of the Earl of Holdernesse."[152] An animated discussion followed the royal message. Lord Hardwicke was in favour of carrying out the King's wish, on the ground that this was the first instance in which the King had interfered in the nomination of ministers, and that resistance might excite ill-will towards the present holders of office; but the Marquis of Rockingham, who realized it was the King's ultimate intention to dismiss the existing Cabinet, urged his colleagues to consider how, if they admitted in February, 1761, that the Earl of Bute was fit to be a Secretary of State, they could say in the following year he was not fit to be Prime Minister.[153] In the end, however, Lord Holdernesse retired in favour of Lord Bute.

This, as Lord Rockingham had foreseen, was regarded by the King as a first step only: he was not content with having placed Bute in the Ministry, he desired to make him Prime Minister. To achieve this object, however, it was necessary to get rid of Pitt, and in this the King had the assistance of the Duke of Newcastle, who scarcely felt himself the chief of the administration that bore his name so long as Pitt, with his great talents and reputation, was in the Ministry. An opportunity soon presented itself. When Pitt, hearing of the "Family Compact" between France and Spain in August, 1761, desired to withdraw the British Ambassador from Madrid, his proposal, supported by Lord Temple and James Grenville, was overruled by Henry Fox, George Grenville, Lord Hardwicke, the Duke of Bedford,[154] and Lord Bute. Finding his influence declining, he threatened to resign, a course that was represented to the King as dangerous to the common weal, "I am determined not to be the only slave in a country," the monarch declared, "where it is my wish to see all the people free." When Pitt found his colleagues had formed a cabal with the object to compel him to retire and that he was powerless to overcome their opposition, he and Lord Temple tendered their resignation on October 5 to the King. The King received Pitt graciously, courteously expressed his regrets at the loss of so able a minister (whom he had assisted to drive from office), expressed approval of the views of his remaining ministers, and in conclusion offered the bestowal of any rewards in the power of the Crown. "I confess, Sire," it is recorded that Pitt replied, overcome by the monarch's kindness, "I had but too much reason to expect your Majesty's displeasure. I did not come prepared for this exceeding goodness; pardon me, Sire, it overpowers, oppresses me." Then, the chroniclers agree, the Great Commoner burst into tears, but before he left the royal presence he had accepted a peerage for his wife and a pension for two lives of £3,000 a year. "It is difficult to say," Walpole remarked, "which exulted most on the occasion, France, Spain, or Lord Bute, for Mr. Pitt was the common enemy of all three."

The behaviour of Pitt's colleagues was resented by the public, and the Corporation of London passed a vote of thanks to the ex-minister, while many who had seen an evil omen in the falling of a large jewel from the crown during the coronation, now declared that their fear had been fulfilled.

> "When first, portentous, it was known,
> Great George had jostled from his crown
>   The brightest diamond there;
> The omen-mongers, one and all,
> Foretold some mischief must befall,
>   Some loss beyond compare.
>
> Some fear this gem is Hanover,
> Whilst others wish to God it were;
>   Each strives the nail to hit
> One guesses that, another this,
> All mighty wise, yet all amiss;
>   For, ah! who thought of Pitt?"[155]

On the other hand, caricaturists and pamphleteers in the pay of Bute exulted in cartoon and verse at the downfall of the Great Commoner, and poured scorn on him for accepting favours at the King's hands.

> "Three thousand a year's no contemptible thing
> To accept from the hands of a patriot king,
> (With thanks, to the bargain, for service and merit),
> Which he, wife and son, all three shall inherit
> With limited honours to *her* and *her heirs*.
> So farewell to old England. *Adieu to all cares.*"[156]

So persistent were the attacks made upon Pitt by Bute's henchmen, who distorted almost out of recognition the story of his resignation, that the ex-minister thought it advisable to meet the misrepresentation by stating the facts in a letter to one of his supporters:—

"Finding, to my great surprise, that the cause and manner of my resigning the seals is grossly misrepresented in the city, as well as that the most gracious and spontaneous remarks of his Majesty's approbation of my services, which marks followed my resignation, have been infamously traduced as a bargain for my forsaking the public, I am under the necessity of declaring the truth of both those facts, in a manner which, I am sure, no gentleman will contradict. A difference of opinion with regard to measures to be taken against Spain, of the highest importance to the honour of the Crown, and to the most essential national interests (and this, founded on what Spain has already done, not on what that court may further intend to do) was the cause of my resigning the seals. Lord Temple and I submitted, in writing, and signed by us, our most humble sentiments to his Majesty; which being overruled by the united opinion of all the rest of the King's servants, I resigned the seals on the 5th of this month, in order not to remain responsible for measures which I was no longer able to guide. Most gracious public marks of his Majesty's approbation followed my resignation. They are unmerited and unsolicited, and I shall ever be proud to have received them from the best of sovereigns."

Pitt's popularity was shown on the Lord Mayor's Day following his resignation when the King, who had been married only two months, went with his Consort in state to the City to dine at the Guildhall. "Men's hopes and fears are strongly agitated at this critical juncture," Alderman Beckford[157] wrote to Pitt; "but all agree universally that you ought to make your appearance at Guildhall on Monday next with Lord Temple; and, upon the maturest reflection, I am clear you ought not to refuse this favour by those who are so sincerely your friends."[158] To this solicitation, backed by the advice of Lord Temple, Pitt yielded, though, as he afterwards admitted, against his better judgment.[159] The King and Queen were received indifferently, Bute was saved from violence only by his guard of prize-fighters, ministers were greeted with cries of "No Newcastle salmon!" but Pitt was welcomed with the greatest enthusiasm, and the mob, a contemporary noted, "clung about every part of the vehicle, hung upon the wheels, hugged his footmen, and even kissed his horses." Though this occurred so early in the reign, it showed a marked difference to the feeling aroused by the King's accession,[160] and it is not to be wondered at that the sovereign, when he referred to this visit to the City, spoke of "the abominable conduct of Mr. Pitt" in joining the procession.

Lord Egremont took Pitt's place, and the Duke of Newcastle made no secret of his delight and relief at having ridded his Cabinet of so overshadowing a subordinate; but the Duke's joy was at least premature, since, as he might have foreseen, the loss of Pitt so greatly weakened the Ministry that within a few months the King was able to remove from the direction of affairs that nobleman of whom George II had said, "He loses an hour every morning, and is running after it the rest of the day," and whom George III now treated with scarcely veiled contempt. "For myself I am the greatest cipher that ever walked at Court. The young King is hardly civil to me, talks to me of nothing, scarcely answers me upon my own Treasury affairs," the Prime Minister wrote on November 7, 1760: and about the same time he complained that, with one exception, he could not remember a single recommendation of his which had taken place since the accession.[161]

Bute, however, gave the minister the *coup de grâce* when the latter strongly advocated the appointment of a certain clergyman to the Archbishopric of York. "If your Grace has so high an opinion of him," said he, "why did you not promote him *when you had the power*?" This was the last straw, and the Duke of Newcastle resigned on May 26, 1762, when Lord Bute became First Lord of the Treasury, with Lord Egremont and George Grenville as Secretaries of State, the incapable and worthless Sir Francis Dashwood,[162] as Chancellor of the Exchequer, and Henry Fox as Leader of the House of Commons. The Admiralty, after the death of Lord Anson, was offered to Lord Halifax[163] who, aspiring to be a Secretary of State, declined the office, and persisted in his refusal until Lord Bute assured him that next to the Treasury it was the most *lucrative* post on the Administration. A humorous description of this incident is given in the "Fables for Grown Gentlemen."

"Close by a kitchen fire, a dog and a cat,
Each a famous politician,
Were meditating as they sat,
Plans and projects of ambition.
By the same fire were set to warm
Fragments of their master's dinner;
   Temptations to alarm
   The frailty of a sinner.
Clear prurient water streamed from Pompey's jaws,
And Tabby looked demure, and lick'd her paws;
   And as two Plenipo's
   For fear of a surprise,
When both have something to propose
Examine one another's eyes;
Or like two maids, though smit by different swains,
In jealous conference o'er a dish of tea,
Pompey and Tabby both cudgelled their brains
Studying each other's physiognomy.
   Pompey endow'd with finer sense,
   Discovered in a cast of Tabby's face,
   A symptom of concupiscence
   Which made it a clear case
When straight applying to the dawning passion,
Pompey addressed her in this fashion:
'Both you and I, with vigilance and zeal,
Becoming faithful dogs, and pious cats,
Have guarded day and night this commonweal
   From robbery and rats.
All that we get for this, heaven knows,
   Is a few bones and many blows;
   Let us no longer fawn and whine,
   Since we have talents and are able,
   Let us impose an equitable fine
     Upon our master's table;
     And, to be brief,
   Let us each choose a single dish,

> I'll be contented with roast beef,
>   Take you that turbot—you love fish.'
>   Thus every dog and cat agrees,
>   When they can settle their own fees.
>   Thus two contending chiefs are seen
>   To agree at last in every measure:
>   One takes the management of the marine,
>   The other of the nation's treasure."

"The new Administration begins tempestuously," Horace Walpole remarked. "My father was not more abused after twenty years than Bute after twenty days. Weekly papers swarm and, like other insects, sting." The feeling against Lord Bute was indeed so great that Dr. Dempster became a popular hero for preaching on December 21, 1760, before the King from Esther v.: "Yet all this availeth nothing, so long as I see Mordecai the Jew sitting at the King's gate"; and caricatures of "Mordecai at the King's gate" were immediately after to be seen in all the print-shops throughout the country; but now Bute was Prime Minister his unpopularity reached its zenith. He was hooted, and sometimes pelted, by the mob: at times even there can be no doubt his life was endangered by the fury of the populace. All England was amused by the story of Miss Chudleigh's retort to her royal mistress, the Princess Dowager, who had administered a rebuke to the maid of honour after the latter had appeared very undressed as Iphigenia at a masked ball at Somerset House: *"Votre Altesse Royale sait que chacune à son—*BUT."[164] Numerous cartoons circulated showing the Princess Dowager and Lord Bute, the latter always wearing a red petticoat, supposed to have been found under very suspicious circumstances; while lampoons were issued in considerable numbers and one enjoyed exceptional popularity: "A letter to her Royal Highness the Princess Dowager of Wales with a word or two concerning Lord Bute and the Talk of the World," with the motto:

> "Hence have the talkers of this populous city
>   A shameful tale to tell for public sport."

Although this scandal was in full cry, it was not that which set every man's hand against the minister, but his inordinate craving for power he was ill-qualified to wield. "Bute made himself immediately Secretary of State, Knight of the Garter,[165] and Privy Purse: he gave an English peerage to his wife; and the reversion of a very lucrative employment for life to his eldest son," Chesterfield complained. "He placed and displaced whom he pleased; gave peerages without number, and pensions without bounds; by those means he proposed to make his ground secure for the permanency of his power."[166] Bute, however, did not sit down quietly under the many attacks of which he was the subject, but responded to his enemies through his band of hired literary bravos. "I am beset with a host of scribblers, and I must acknowledge that I can discern great talent in some of their productions," he wrote in

February, 1761. "The fire must not be allowed to spread too far, or I know not where its devastations will end. I am at a loss at present how to stem the tide of popularity which sets in at present so strongly against the court party. The King is much disposed at times to break out very violently in his objections to certain measures, but I hope I shall succeed eventually.... Pitt got the better of me in the [debate on the] Speech which his Majesty delivered from the throne, in which, as you will have read, he is made to declare that he is determined to carry on the war with vigour. We have it now in agitation to make him say quite the contrary, for we are resolved to have a peace.... I am informed of a work which is now in the press, entitled *Le Montagnard Parvenu*, of which I contrive to obtain the sheets as they are printed. The author knows more than I wish him to know; he must have been oftener behind the curtain than I suspected; it must be met by corresponding talent; the King must not see it.... I am, however, by no means without literary talent on my side; most of *our* best authors are wholly devoted to me, and I have laid the foundation for gaining Robertson,[167] by employing him for the King, in writing the history of England; he must be pensioned."[168]

Some credit is due to Bute for his patronage of literature. He pensioned Robertson, and John Home, the author of the play, "Douglas," which is now remembered only by the passage beginning "My name is Norval," and Mallet, [169] Murphy,[170] Macpherson,[171] Tobias Smollett and Dr. Johnson, to the last of whom it was stated specifically that the award was made, "not for anything you are to do, but for what you have done."[172] But if in some cases a pension was bestowed for merit, and for merit alone, these were the exception, for bribery was as much employed by Bute as it had been by Walpole, and once again the Paymaster's office was the *rendezvous* for those Members of Parliament whose votes were for sale.[173]

Bute came into power determined to bring about a peace, but he found it impossible forthwith to achieve his object, and, indeed, as Pitt had prophesied, he was compelled to declare war against Spain. He was much chagrined at having to act in direct violation of his wishes, but the war, which was as popular as it was successful, might in some degree have consoled him, had not the country given the credit to Pitt, who, before leaving office, had made preparations for the campaign. On December 22, 1762, the preliminaries of peace were discussed in the House of Commons, when Pitt, though suffering agonies from gout, appeared, his leg swathed in flannel, to protest against the treaty, the terms of which aroused general dissatisfaction, and it was declared that the Duke of Bedford, the English negotiator, had sold his country, and that the Princess Dowager and the Prime Minister had shared in the spoil. "Your patrons wanted an Ambassador who would submit to make concessions without daring to insist upon any honourable condition for his sovereign," said Junius. "Their business required a man who had as little feeling for his own dignity as for the welfare of his country; and they found him in the first rank of the nobility. Belleisle, Goree, Guadaloupe, St. Louis, Martinique, the Fishery, and Havana are glorious monuments of your Grace's talents for negotiation. My Lord, we are too well acquainted with your pecuniary character to think it possible that so many public sacrifices should be made without some private compensation. Your conduct carries with it an internal evidence beyond all the legal proofs of a court of justice."[174] The House of Commons, however, signified its approval of the treaty by 319 to 65 votes; whereupon the Princess Dowager exclaimed in triumph: "Now my son *is* King of England."[175] The King was delighted, the Queen gave a ball in honour of the victory of the Court, and Bute declared that he wished for no other epitaph than one in which he should be described as the adviser of this peace—which prompted an unkind epigram:

> "Say, when will England be from faction freed?
> When will domestic quarrels cease?
> Ne'er till that wished-for epitaph we read,
> 'Here lies the man that made the peace.'"

The cyder tax, which Bute forced through Parliament to defray the heavy expenses of the negotiations for peace, threw even his previous unpopularity into insignificance, and his endeavours to persuade the City of London not to present a petition against the tax, by promising to repeal it the next year, was met with the reply, "My Lord, we know not that you will be minister next year." To the general surprise, Bute's resignation was announced on April 3, 1763, when with him retired Fox, who entered the Upper House as Baron Holland, and Dashwood, who succeeded his uncle as Baron le Despencer.

Bute's resignation was said by his friends to be the natural sequence of his policy, and to have been determined before he accepted the seals of office. The noble patriot, so his henchmen insisted, had seen his country wasted by a pernicious, unnecessary war, and he had secured the office of prime minister in order to, and solely in order to, achieve peace. This done, they continued, his self-imposed task was complete, and he withdrew from public affairs, "without place or pension, disdaining to touch those tempting spoils which lay at his feet."[176] These reasons for the surrender of office cannot, in the light of present knowledge, be accepted. Bute retired owing to dissension in his Cabinet. Indeed, for this there is his own admission. "Single in a cabinet of my own forming; no aid in the House of Lords to support me, except two peers [Lords Denbigh and Pomfret]; both the Secretaries of State silent; and the Lord Chief Justice, whom I myself brought into office, voting for me, yet speaking against me; the ground I tread upon is so hollow, that I am afraid, not only of falling myself, but of involving my Royal Master in my ruin. It is time for me to retire."[177]

The failings of Lord Bute have already been discussed, and in taking leave of him some mention must be made of his good qualities. It has been said that his besetting fault was a lust of power, his great weakness inability to use the power which his intrigues secured him; but he was a good husband, a kind father, and, what more concerns the public, a brave man, for he faced exceptional unpopularity without flinching, and, according to his lights, honest. It would be objectionable to say to-day of a living English statesman that he was honest in financial matters, for it is inconceivable that any other would be tolerated; but it must not be forgotten that the tone of political men was then very different. In Bute's day gross immorality was no bar to employment in the highest offices of state, nor was overt dishonesty a disqualification. We have seen how Lord Halifax was persuaded to accept the Admiralty because of the opportunities to acquire wealth, and it is notorious that the great and able Henry Fox accumulated a vast fortune during his tenure of office of Paymaster-General. Dashwood, who, according to Walpole, was a vulgar fool, who "with the familiarity and phrase of a fishwife, introduced the humours of Wapping behind the veil of the Treasury," was a thoroughly vicious scoundrel; Rigby, whose accusers have exhausted the terms of vituperation, was also a Paymaster-General, and left half-a-million of money; Grafton, a great-grandson of Charles II by the Duchess of Cleveland, was a notorious profligate. The list might be continued until it embraced a large proportion of the politicians on both sides. No reproach of this sort clings to Bute, who did not for himself appropriate public monies, and if the cynic contends that this was because he had no temptation to be dishonest, having married a wife who brought him £25,000 a year and nearly a quarter of a million in the funds, the fact must not be ignored that many of those who plunged their hands into the country's purse were possessed of greater wealth.

From a drawing by Jno. Smith
WINDSOR CASTLE

CHAPTER IX

THE COURT OF GEORGE III

Even before he ascended the throne George III had determined that his Court should be very different from that of his grandfather, and when he came into his kingdom he began at once a very drastic process of purification. He was a religious man, somewhat narrow in his views, and he held sacred things in great respect. At the coronation, after he had been anointed and crowned, when the Archbishop of Canterbury came to hand him down from the throne to receive the Sacrament, he told them he would not go to the Lord's Supper and partake of that ordinance with the crown on his head. The Archbishop of Canterbury did not know if it might be removed, and, after consulting the Bishop of Rochester, told the King neither could say if there was any order in the service for receiving communion with or without the crown. "Then there ought to be," said the monarch, and himself laid aside the crown.[178] Indeed he held very strong views as to the Sacrament, and when in 1805 Lord Chesterfield[179] prior to an Installation asked if the new Knights of the Garter would be required to take it, "No, My Lord," he replied severely, "the Holy Sacrament is not to be profaned by our Gothic institutions. Even at my coronation I was very unwilling to take it, but they told me it was indispensable. As it was, I took off the bauble from my head before I approached the Altar."[180]

George had this deep feeling for religion from his childhood, and before he was six years old had without direction learnt by heart several pages of Doddridge's "Principles of the Christian Religion"; while, from the time he grew up to the end of his life, he devoted one hour in the early morning to reading the Scriptures and to meditation. He was well acquainted with the works of Andrews, Sanderson and Sherlock, and asked a fashionable preacher of the day if he, too, were acquainted with them. "No, please your Majesty, my reading is all modern. The writers of whom you speak are now obsolete, though I doubt not they might have been very well at the time." The King looked at him, thinking of the man's own sermons, and replied: "There were giants on earth in those days."[181] One day George missed an under-gardener, and inquired as to the reason of his absence. "Please your Majesty, he is of late so very troublesome with his religion and he is always talking about it." "Is he dishonest? Does he neglect his work?" "No, your Majesty, he is very honest. I have nothing to say against him for that." "Then send for him again. Why should he be turned off? Call me Defender of the Faith!" he thundered. "*Defender of the Faith!*—and turn away a man for his religion!"

George III was not so bigoted but that he would visit a Quaker, and he and his consort witnessed the Lord Mayor's Show in 1761 from the house of Robert Barclay, one of the sect; and he could speak kindly of Nonconformists. On one occasion at Windsor he saw a maid-servant in tears and learnt that her distress was occasioned by the refusal of a superior to allow her to attend a dissenting meeting, whereupon he sent for the housekeeper and admonished her severely: "I will suffer no persecution during my reign!" "The Methodists are a quiet good kind of people and will disturb nobody; and if I can learn that any persons in my employment disturb them, they shall be immediately dismissed," he said when an attempt was made to interrupt the service at a Methodist chapel; and when a Bible Society was formed at Windsor, and the name of the Independent minister omitted, he desired that the name of "that good man" should without delay be added. But though George III could tolerate Nonconformists, on the other hand nothing could induce him to abate his prejudice against the Roman Catholics, and when urged to make concessions to them: "Tell me who took the coronation oath, did you or I? Dundas, let me have no more of your Scotch sophistry. I took the oath, and I must keep it."

After George's accession Dr. Thomas Wilson, Prebendary of Westminster, thought, by flattering him in a sermon delivered in the Chapel Royal, to ingratiate himself with the new King, only to be summoned to receive, to his great surprise, a stern rebuke: those who preached before him, the monarch warned Dr. Wilson, must remember "I go to church to hear God praised and not myself." George had, indeed, a high ideal for those in clerical orders, and this he enforced on all classes. "I could not help giving you the notification of the grief and concern with which my breast was affected at receiving an authentic information that routs have made their way into your palace," he wrote to Archbishop Cornwallis, when in 1772 he was informed by the Countess of Huntingdon that the prelate's wife had given a ball. "At the same time I must signify to you my sentiments on this subject, which hold these levities and vain dissipations as utterly inexpedient, if not unlawful, to pass in a residence for many centuries devoted to Divine studies, religious retirement, and the extensive exercise of charity and benevolence—I add, in a place where so many of your predecessors have led their lives in such sanctity as has thrown lustre upon the pure religion they professed and adorned. From the dissatisfaction with which you must perceive I behold these improprieties, not to speak in harsher terms, and still more pious principles, I trust you will suppress them immediately; so that I may not have occasion to show any further marks of displeasure, or to interpose in a different manner. May God take your Grace into His Almighty protection."

"I wish that every poor child in my dominion shall be able to read his Bible,"[182] he said rightly enough; but sometimes his fervour led him into excesses, such as the striking out in his copy of the Prayer-Book in the prayer for the Royal Family the words "our most Gracious King and Governor," and substituting an "unworthy sinner." It was this and similar examples of misdirected fervour that prompted Byron to write:

> "All I saw further, in the last confusion,
> Was, that King George slipped into Heaven for one;
> And when the tumult dwindled to a calm,
> I left him practising the hundredth psalm."[183]

One of the first acts of the King was to issue a proclamation for the "encouragement of piety and virtue, and for preventing and punishing of vice, profaneness, and immorality," which was especially commended to the notice of "judges, mayors, sheriffs, justices of the peace, and all other our officers and ministers, both ecclesiastical and civil."

"GEORGE R.

"We most seriously and religiously considering that it is an indispensable duty on us to be careful above all things to preserve and advance the honour and service of Almighty God, and to discourage and suppress all vice, profaneness, debauchery, and immorality, which are so highly displeasing to God, so great a reproach to our religion and government, and (by means of the frequent ill examples of the practices thereof) have so fatal a tendency to the corruption of many of our loving subjects, otherwise religiously and virtuously disposed, and which (if not timely remedied) may justly draw down the Divine vengeance on us and our kingdoms: we also humbly acknowledging that we cannot expect the blessing and goodness of Almighty God (by Whom Kings reign and on which we entirely rely) to make our reign happy and prosperous to ourself and to our people, without a religious observance of God's holy laws: to the intent thereof that religion, piety, and good manners may (according to our most hearty desire) flourish and increase under our administration and government, we have thought fit, by the advice of our Privy Council, to issue this our royal proclamation, and do hereby declare our royal purpose and resolution to discountenance and punish all manner of vice, profaneness, and immorality, in all persons of whatsoever degree or quality, within this our realm, and particularly in such as are employed near our royal person; and that for the encouragement of religion and morality, we will, upon all occasions, distinguish persons of piety and virtue, by marks of our royal favour. And we do expect and require that all persons of honour, or in place of authority, will give good example of their own virtue and piety, and to their utmost contribute to the discountenancing persons of dissolute and debauched lives, that they, being reduced by that means to shame and contempt for their loose and evil actions and behaviour, may be therefore also enforced the sooner to reform their ill habits and practices, and that the visible displeasure of good men towards them may (as far as it is possible) supply what the laws (probably) cannot altogether prevent. And we do hereby enjoin and prohibit all our loving subjects, of what degree or quality soever, from playing on the Lord's day at dice, cards, or any other game whatsoever; and we do hereby require and command them, and every one of them, decently and reverently to attend the worship of God on every Lord's-day, on pain of our highest displeasure, and being proceeded against with the utmost rigour that may be by law...."

Practical measures followed this proclamation, and first, as was to be expected from so regular a church-goer, George announced that the Sabbath Day must not be profaned even by so harmless an entertainment as a reception, and abolished the Sunday Drawing-rooms. This was followed by the discouragement of gambling at Court. When George discovered that at the Twelfth Night celebrations at St. James's Palace hazard was played for heavy stakes, he was horrified. First, he restricted the number of tables, later limited the hours of play, and subsequently refused to permit this amusement in his palaces. Then cards were instituted, only in turn to be forbidden, and it was announced that no game for money would be permitted among officials, under penalty of forfeiting their situations.[184]

It is an axiom that people cannot be made virtuous by proclamation, yet it is conceivable that those persons who were not moved to laughter by the exhortation to be good might appreciate it as an earnest of the King's intention to exact a standard of conduct higher than had been previously attained; and some acceptable result might have followed had the Court been popular, for, if the courtiers obeyed their master's behest, it is probable that those in lower ranks might follow the exalted example. Things began well. "For the King himself, he seems all good-nature, and wishing to satisfy everybody," Walpole wrote at the beginning of the reign. "All his speeches are obliging—I saw him yesterday, and was surprised to find that the *levée* room had lost so entirely the air of the lion's den. This sovereign does not stand in one spot, with his eyes royally fixed on the ground, and dropping bits of German news; he walked about and spoke to everybody; I saw him afterwards on the throne, where he is graceful and genteel, sits with dignity, and reads his answers well."

After the royal marriage, however, the good start was not followed up: the Court became the dullest and dreariest place conceivable and was soon attended only by those whose duties compelled them to attend. "The Court, independent of politics, makes the strangest figure," Walpole wrote to Lord Hertford not very long after the accession. "The Drawing-rooms are abandoned. Lady Buckingham was the only woman there on Sunday se'nnight. In short, one hears of nothing but dissatisfaction, which, in the city, rises almost to treason." Lord Holland, too, noted the prevalent feeling. "A young, civil, virtuous, good-natured King might naturally be expected to have such a degree of popularity as should for years defend the most exceptionable Favourite," he wrote in September, 1762. "But, which I can't account for, his Majesty from the very beginning was not popular. And now, because Lord Talbot[185] has prevented him from being cheated to the shameful degree that has been usual in his kitchen, they make prints treating his Majesty as they would a notorious old miser."[186]

Lord Talbot was Lord Steward of the Household and his appointment was not popular. "As neither gravity, rank, abilities, nor morals could be adduced to counterbalance such exaltation, no wonder it caused very unfavourable comments," was Walpole's opinion. "As the Court knew that the measures it had in contemplation could only be carried by money, every stratagem was invented to curtail the common expenses of the palace. As these fell into the province of the Lord Steward, nothing was heard of but cooks cashiered and kitchens shut up. Even the Maids of Honour, who did not expect rigours from a great officer of Lord Talbot's complexion, were reduced to complain of the abridgment of their allowance for breakfast."[187] The drastic changes in Lord Talbot's department brought down upon the nobleman a diatribe from Wilkes. "I much admire many of his Lordship's new regulations, especially those for the royal kitchen. I approve of the discharge of so many turnspits and cooks, who were grown of little use. It was high time to put an end to that too great indulgence in eating and drinking, which went by the name of Old English Hospitality, when the House of Commons had granted a poor niggardly Civil List of only £800,000."[188]

From a print dated 1762

THE KITCHEN METAMORPHOZ'D

The fact of the matter was the King was not possessed of those qualities that make for popularity. At times he showed a certain graciousness, as when at some watering-place where he went with the Queen, "We must walk about for two or three days to please these good people," he said, alluding to the crowds that assembled to see him, "and then *we may walk about to please ourselves*." Indeed, on the afternoons of Sundays and royal birthdays when the Court was at Windsor and the weather was fine, the King and Queen with their family walked on the Terrace, which was usually crowded with people of rank and fashion, and made so pretty a picture that many came from London to see the sight. In the country George was affable, especially with humble folk. At Weymouth he passed a field where, although it was harvest time, only one woman was at work, and, surprised by this neglect of work, he asked where were the other labourers. The woman said they had gone to see the King, and added: "I would not give a pin to see him. Besides, the fools will lose a day's work by it, and that is more than I can afford to do. I have five children to work for." "Well, then," said his Majesty, putting some money in her hands, "you may tell your companions who are gone to see the King, that the *King came to see you*."[189] Occasionally he would pay a compliment, as on one occasion at a review at Winchester when David Garrick, having dismounted and lost his horse, which, alarmed by the noise, had broken away, exclaimed, "A horse! a horse! my kingdom for a horse," the King turned round, "I thought I could not be mistaken, Mr. Garrick," he said, "your delivery of Shakespeare can never pass unnoticed."[190] More frequently, however, his remarks were tactless, as in his conversation with a Yorkshireman at a *levée*, "I suppose you are going back to Yorkshire, Mr. Stanhope? A very ugly county, Yorkshire!" "Oh, sir!" said Stanhope, outraged in his tenderest feelings, "we always consider Yorkshire a very picturesque county." "What, what, what!" cried the King, who evidently had not sought the soft answer that turns away anger. "A coal-pit a picturesque object! What, what, what! Yorkshire coalpits, picturesque! Yorkshire a picturesque county!"[191]

Yet, though George neither as lad nor man possessed wit, at times he gave proofs of an unexpected vein of humour. Thus, when he inquired who was the owner of a newly erected palatial house, and was told it had been built by his Majesty's card-maker, "Indeed," quoth he, "then this man's cards have all turned up trumps." On another occasion when he had purchased a horse, the dealer handed him a large piece of parchment with the remark, "The animal's pedigree, Sire." "No, no," said the monarch, handing it back. "Keep it, my good man, 'twill do as well for the next horse you sell," which shows more knowledge of the world than is usually accredited to the speaker. One day Colonel Manners, who was in high favour at Court, sought an interview. "Let him in," the King replied, "he is not only Manners, but good manners." When at the end of March, 1781, Lord Bateman waited on him to ask at what hour his Majesty would have the stag-hounds turned out, "My Lord, I cannot exactly answer that," he replied, having just bestowed the Mastership on the Marquis of Carnarvon,[192] "but I can inform you that your Lordship was turned out an hour ago." More amusing is the message he sent to a Jacobite who would not take the oath of allegiance or acknowledge him as King of England—"Carry my compliments to him—but—what—stop—no—he may perhaps not receive my compliments as King of England. Give him the Elector of Hanover's compliments, and tell him that he respects the steadiness of his principles."

When Lord Chief Baron Macdonald, a great snuff-taker, and Mr. Baron Graham, an inveterate talker, were sitting in the Westminster court, "The Court of Exchequer," remarked the King, "has a snuffbox at one end and a chatterbox at the other."[193] To Lord Kenyon, a very violent-tempered man, he said: "My Lord, I hear that since you have been in the King's Bench, you have *lost your temper*. You know my great regard for you, and I may therefore venture to tell you I am glad to hear it."[194] Humorous, too, was his remark, *à propos* of George Selwyn's love of horrors. Selwyn was present at a *levée*, and withdrew after George had spoken to him, although it was known the monarch was to confer the honour of knighthood upon a country squire who had come to Court to present an Address. "The King afterwards, in the closet, expressed his astonishment to the Groom-in-Waiting," wrote Storer to Lord Auckland, "that Mr. Selwyn should not wish to see the ceremony of making a new knight, observing that it looked so like an *execution* that he took it for granted Mr. Selwyn would have stayed to see it."[195]

An amusing incident has also been related by Colonel Landmann when George III was at Weymouth. "The King had taken off one of his military white gloves, and in dropping the ends of his sash, he also at the same time dropped the glove, upon which, not only General Garth, but several others nearest to the King, scrambled for the glove on the ground, in order to mark their zeal and attention to his Majesty; but the King, desirous of recovering his fallen glove without having to thank any one for it, or perhaps wishing to display his activity, also attempted to seize it, in which he succeeded. On rising, the King's cane slipped from his hold, and again the King was the successful candidate for the prize. Now the sensation which the scrambling for the glove and then for the stick had created amongst the vast concourse of spectators was increased to an uncontrollable degree by the falling off of the King's hat, for the capture of which an increased number of competitors presented themselves, whose ambition to serve his Majesty greatly retarded its restitution.

"Colonel Campbell, at length, had the good fortune to rescue this from the hands of two members of the King's household, who were struggling with each other for victory; whilst the King, holding out his hands for his property, his face, in consequence of his stooping, as red as his coat, exclaimed: 'Never mind about the honour of the thing, never mind, never mind; give me my hat, give me my hat; there,' as the King received his hat, 'thank you—thank you all alike—you all picked it up—yes, yes,—all, all, all—you all picked it up.'

"The King, during the latter part of this contest, laughed most heartily, in which the whole of the *cortège* surrounding his Majesty immediately joined, throwing off all restraint."[196]

One of the best stories concerning George III has since been told in many forms of other persons. The King and his eldest son assisted a countryman whose cart had stuck in a rut near Windsor, and, after literally putting their shoulders to the wheel, they gave him respectively half-a-guinea and a guinea. The driver was puzzled to receive a larger coin from the Prince of Wales than from the monarch, who heard of the man's perplexity, and, meeting him again some time after, explained the matter: "Friend, I find you cannot account for my son being more generous than I; but you should consider I have a large family to provide for; he is but a single man, and has nobody to provide for but himself."

Even better than this was his remark after his recovery in 1789, when he heard that "Old Q." had gone over to the Opposition: "For once the old jockey has run on the wrong side of the post." This occasional sense of humour was rarely carried into the domain of affairs of state, but one instance when humour and justice combined has been preserved. Picking a pocket was not a capital felony, but in those days taking anything privily from the person, of the value of one shilling, was punishable with death. George abolished for all practical purposes this absurd distinction, for when the warrant for the execution of a pickpocket was brought for his signature, he refused to sign it, declaring there was no difference between the offences. "I had always understood," said he, "that the very essence of picking a pocket was, that it should be done as much as possible without the knowledge of the party."[197]

The King had a great sense of regal dignity, and, when outraged, could administer a rebuke with an air that rendered it crushing. When Lord Kingsale, in the exercise of the privilege bestowed by King John to wear his hat in the royal presence, remained covered, not for an instant, but throughout a Court, in the presence of the King and Queen, "My Lord Kingsale," said the monarch, "you are entitled to remain covered in the presence of your sovereign, but not in the presence of a lady." Again, when Addington quarrelled with Pitt, he went to surrender the key of the Council box that he held as Lord President of the Council, but the King declined angrily to receive it: "You must not give it to me, but to Lord Hawkesbury"; and when the retiring minister begged to be excused on the ground that Lord Hawkesbury and he were not on speaking terms, "that," said George, "was no concern of his."

George III took himself with the greatest seriousness, not only in matters of importance, but also in the most trivial details of ceremony, and when any change in etiquette was mooted, met the suggestion with the stereotyped reply, "I will have no innovations in my time." He could not bring himself ever to unbend even with ministers who were brought into daily contact with him, and during the interview, however long it might be, he would stand, and so prevent the minister from taking a seat. Indeed, on one occasion when Pitt was suffering from gout, George kept him standing for two hours, though well aware of the statesman's infirmity, for two days later he said to him he hoped he had not suffered by standing so long on Monday. And Pitt was overcome by this gracious inquiry and told his friends, "His Majesty is the greatest courtier in the country".[198]

It was not only ministers, however, who suffered in this way, for on one occasion Mrs. Siddons, who was summoned to read a play before their Majesties, was kept on her feet until she nearly fell from fatigue.

> "Ready to drop to earth, she must have sunk,
> But for a child that at the hardship shrunk—
> A little *prince*, who marked her situation,
> Thus, pitying, pour'd a tender exclamation:
> 'La! Mrs. Siddons is quite faint indeed,
> How pale! I'm sure she cannot read:
> She somewhat wants, her spirits to repair,

> And would, I'm sure, be happy in a *chair.*'
> What follow'd? Why, the r-y-l pair arose
> Surly enough, one fairly may suppose!
> And to a room adjoining made retreat,
> To let her, for one moment, *steal* a seat."[199]

When George III "put on the King," Beckford said, "he was the personification of dignity," and "no man could stand before him";[200] while the impression he made on Johnson is well known. "Sir, they may talk of the King as they will, but he is the finest gentleman I have ever seen," the doctor said to Barnard, the librarian; and supplemented this to Langton: "Sir, his manners are those of as fine a gentleman as we may suppose Louis the Fourteenth or Charles the Second."[201] This regal dignity was, however, not always sustained in private. "The oscillations of his body, the precipitations of his questions, none of which, it was said, would wait for an answer, and the hurry of his articulation"[202] were so many faults; and the famous "What? what?" with which he concluded his sentences were irritating to a degree. "His Majesty is multifarious in his questions," said Johnson, "but thank God he answers them all himself." The King was no fool, however, and, as Wraxall was at pains to point out, "his understanding, solid and sedate, qualified him admirably for business," though it was neither of a brilliant nor imposing description; but he had in him a great vein of folly.

Now, the dignity of a foolish man usually furnishes fit subject for mirth, and the King's reputation for stupidity, which originated in his early years, grew confirmed as time went on. No story, however seemingly absurd, was rejected as untrue by his loyal subjects, who, perhaps, found their greatest pleasure in this direction, in the well-known anecdote of the King and the apple dumpling.

> "Once upon a time, a monarch, tired with whooping,
>   Whipping and spurring,
>   Happy in worrying
> A poor defenceless, harmless buck
> (The horse and rider wet as muck),
> From his high consequence and wisdom stooping,
>   Enter'd, through curiosity, a cot.
>   Where sat a poor old woman and her pot.
>
> "The wrinkled, blear-ey'd, good, old granny,
>   In this same cot, illum'd by many a cranny,
>   Had finish'd apple dumplings for her pot:
>   In tempting row the naked dumplings lay,
>   When, lo! the monarch, in his usual way,
> Like lightning spoke, 'What's this? what's this? what? what?'
>
> "Then taking up a dumpling in his hand,
>   His eyes with admiration did expand—
>   And oft did Majesty the dumpling grapple:
>   ''Tis monstrous, monstrous hard, indeed,' he cried:
> 'What makes it, pray, so hard?'—The dame reply'd,

Low curtseying, 'Please, your Majesty, the apple.'

"'Very astonishing, indeed! strange thing!'
(Turning the dumpling round, rejoin'd the King).
"'Tis most extraordinary then, all this is,
It beats Piretti's conjuring all to pieces,
Strange I should never of a dumpling dream,
But, goody, tell me where, where, where's the seam?'
"'Sir, there's no seam,' quoth she, 'I never knew[Pg 190]
That folks did apple dumplings *sew*'—
'No,' cry'd the staring monarch with a grin,
'How, how the devil got the apple in?'

"On which the dame the curious scheme revealed
By which the apple lay so sly concealed;
Which made the Solomon of Britain start:
Who to the Palace with full steam repaired,
And Queen and Princesses so beauteous scared,
All with the wonders of the Dumpling Art.

"There did he labour one whole week, to show
The wisdom of an Apple-Dumpling maker:
And, lo! so deep was Majesty in dough,
The Palace seemed the lodging of a Baker."[203]

The King's folly was most clearly seen in his pronouncements upon scientific questions. He had some liking for mechanics, and, it is said, directed the construction of some interesting clocks; but certainly, apart from mechanics, he was wofully ignorant, and as obstinate as he was ignorant. "Well, I suppose all your chickens are dead," he said to Beckford, alluding to the fact that his house was roofed with copper, an experiment which the King had declared must infallibly kill everything under the roof with verdigris.[204] George took an active part in the question which arose about 1778, whether lightning conductors, which at this time were ordered to be placed near all the powder magazines, should have blunted or pointed ends. A great dispute was raging: Sir John Pringle, President of the Royal Society, Dr. Franklin, and many men of light and leading advocating points, a view controverted by Sir Joseph Banks and some others. It was obviously a question for scientific experts, but the King, as a wit put it, "being rather *partial* to blunt conductors," thought to put an end to the matter by giving his peremptory decision, and announcing to the world the superiority of nobs. Not content with carrying out his theory in the lightning conductors at Buckingham House, he desired Sir John Pringle to publish his belief as the opinion of the Royal Society! Of course to this amazing demand, there could be but one answer, and Sir John regretted "it was not in his power to reverse the order of nature."

Caricature by R. Newton
LEARNING TO MAKE APPLE DUMPLINGS

For art George had some liking, thus forming an agreeable contrast to his two predecessors who detested "bainting and boetry," but unfortunately his taste was quite uninformed and his critical faculties negligible: he preferred Benjamin West to Reynolds, and Peter Pindar "wept over the hard fate of Prince Octavius and Prince Augustus, children of our Most Glorious Sovereign," whose portraits had, by royal command, been painted by West.

"Ghost of Octavius! tell the bard,
    And thou, Augustus, us'd so *hard*,
Why West hath murdered you, my tender lambs?
    You bring to mind vile Richard's deed,
    Who bid your royal cousins bleed,
For which the world the tyrant's mem'ry damns.

"West, I must own thou dost inherit
    Some portion of the painting spirit;
But trust me—not extraordinary things—
    Some merit thou must surely own
    By getting up so near the throne,
And gaining whispers from the best of Kings."[205]

The King also delighted in Beattie, who was his and his consort's favourite poet.

> "... Sweet Poesy exalts her voice,
> MacOssian sings, and Homer's halls rejoice,
> One lazy tenor Beattie's bag-pipe keeps,
> And tragic Home most lamentably weeps.
> The Monarch's favourites, and the Muses' too!
> 'Whawr, Bratons, whawr's yore *Woolly Shockspare noo!*'"[206]

However, to the best of his ability, George admired, and if when shown some of Blake's drawings he cried, "What—what—what! Take them away, take them away!" and if he thought Shakespeare "sad stuff," on the other hand it is to his credit that he took much interest in the foundation of the Royal Academy, and, though he did not desire that Reynolds should be President, yet he sanctioned the appointment and knighted the painter. In his respect for letters he conceived the idea to establish an Order of Minerva for eminent writers and scientists. "The knights were to take rank after the Knights of the Bath, and to sport a straw-coloured ribbon and a star of sixteen points. But there was such a row among the *literati* as to the persons who should be appointed, that the plan was given up, and Minerva and her star never came down amongst us."[207] He accumulated a fine library that George IV, when he found he might not sell it, gave to the British Museum; but he was probably entirely ignorant of his acquisitions, though he had a fondness for the exterior of books, and it is to his credit that he instructed his librarian "never to bid a farthing against a scholar, or professor, or against any person of moderate means, desiring a particular volume for his own use."[208]

George liked to think himself a patron of art and artists, but it is hinted he was not always inspired by the right motive, as when he found a place for Gibbon as a Lord of Trade:

> "King George in a fright,
>   Lest Gibbon should write
>   The Hist'ry of England's disgrace,
> Thought no way so sure
>   His pen to secure
>   As to give the historian a place."

The royal patronage was certainly not exercised on the heroic scale. Thus, Richard Paton was commanded to bring to Kew for their Majesties' inspection naval pictures intended for St. Petersburg, and he obeyed the summons, at a cost of fifty pounds for carriage, for which he was repaid only with thanks; and it was the payment by the King of twenty-five pounds for a picture, the market price of which was four times that amount, painted by a friend of Dr. Wolcot, that brought down upon the monarch the many vigorous onslaughts by that keen though coarse satirist.[209]

On another occasion the Queen was persuaded to sit to young Thomas Lawrence. "The poor young fellow was naturally inexperienced in the ways of a Court, and the manner in which her Majesty treated him was not with her usual kind consideration. She declined to give him a last sitting for the ornaments, as it was too much trouble, but eventually was prevailed upon to allow Mrs. Papendiek to act as her deputy. No money was paid. The King told him to remove it to town, and have it engraved. When that was done, the portrait was to be sent to Hanover, and then the King proposed to pay. But Lawrence had no money, and could not risk the engraving at his own expense."[210] The picture, therefore, remained in his studio, and was sold with others after his death.

Even royalty itself was not able to induce the King to put aside his dislike of spending money, for when the Empress of Russia asked for a portrait of himself by Reynolds, the monarch, with "laudable royal economy," as the satirist put it, went, not to Reynolds, but to an inexpensive portrait-painter.

> "I'm told, and I believe the story,
> That a fam'd Queen of Northern brutes,
> A gentlewoman of *prodigious* glory,
> Whom every sort of epithet *well suits*;
> Whose husband *dear*, just happening to *provoke* her,
> Was shov'd to heaven upon a *red-hot poker*!
> Sent to a *certain* King, not King of *France*,
> Desiring by Sir Joshua's hand his phiz,
> What did the royal quiz?
> Why, *damned genteelly*, sat to Mr. Dance."[211]

Certainly on no occasion made public did George III ever show a royal generosity. He saved his old master, Goupy, from a debtor's prison, and appointed his fencing master Redman, who had fallen upon evil days, a Poor Knight of Windsor; he released a man who had been imprisoned twelve years in Dorchester Jail for a debt of £100 by paying that amount; and one day, having taken shelter in a cottage where a joint was suspended before the fire by a string, he left two guineas behind him to "buy a jack."

"I never considered the King as munificent," Lord Carlisle remarked; "when he gave the kettledrums costing £1,500 to the Blues, he was deranged. Before his illness he stopped all the hunt to give an old man something for opening a gate at Bray Wick: after a long search for his purse he produced from it a penny and bestowed it on the man. He gave a *fête* in the Castle to all the Eton school boys. It consisted of a very long concert of sacred music with nothing to eat or drink."[212]

From an old print

THE KING RELIEVING PRISONERS IN
DORCHESTER GAOL

It was not so much that George III was not good-natured, but that he lacked the imagination that might have assisted him to a more worthy generosity. He could never divest himself of a care for trifling sums of money, and while he would authorize, nay encourage, the spending of millions to further some matter upon which he had set his heart, he would sit at home and work out the cost of his son's household to a halfpenny,[213] and take great care that his agricultural hobby should show a balance on the right side, which last consideration aroused again and again the ire of Peter Pindar.

"The modern bard, quoth Tom, sublimely sings
   Of sharp and prudent economic kings,
Who rams, and ewes, and lambs, and bullocks feed.
   And pigs of every sort of breed:

"Of Kings who pride themselves on fruitful sows;
   Who sell skim milk, and keep a guard so stout
   To drive the geese, the thievish rascals, out,
That ev'ry morning us'd to suck the cows;

   "Of Kings who cabbages and carrots plant
   For such as wholesome vegetables want;
   Who feed, too, poultry for the people's sake,

Then send it through the villages in carts,
To cheer (how wondrous kind!) the hungry hearts
Of such as *only pay* for what they take."[214]

From a drawing by Isaac Cruikshank, 1791
SUMMER AMUSEMENTS AT FARMER GEORGE'S

The reason for the unpopularity of the Court may be traced, not to the King's lack of appreciation of what was best in art and letters, not even to his stupidity, but to the lack of wisdom in the sovereigns who, in their zeal for reform, carried their love of decorum to excess (although the Queen's Puritanism was not so deep but that she could for her own ends aid and abet such a frail, designing baggage as Lady Jersey[215]), and to a parsimony unpardonable when exercised in conjunction with a large Civil List.[216] Their miserly tendencies were noted and commented upon with disgust at the Queen's first party, given on November 26, 1762, a "gingerbread affair," which, including the ladies-and-gentlemen-in-waiting, did not consist of more than a baker's dozen of couples. On this occasion, though dancing began before seven o'clock and went on uninterrupted till long after midnight, there was no supper, an omission that furnished Lord Chesterfield with the opportunity for a *bon-mot* in a subsequent conversation as to possible additions to the peerage on the King's next birthday. "I suppose," said some one, "there will be no dukes made." "Oh, yes," said Lord Chesterfield, "there is to be *one*. Lord Talbot is to be created Duke Humphrey, and there is to be no table kept at Court but his!" Those who attended the royal functions fully appreciated this reference to "dining with Duke Humphrey"; and Peter Pindar voiced the public feeling in his "Odes to Kien Long":

> "The pocket is a very serious matter,
> *Small beer* allayeth thirst—nay, *simple water*.
> The splendour of a chase, or feast, or ball,
> Though strong, are passing momentary rays—

> The lustre of a little hour; that's all—
> While *guineas* with *eternal* splendour blaze."

The lack of hospitality shown to those who attended at Court was combined with an equal penury in connexion with those who were summoned to amuse the royal circle, and of some disgraceful examples of this unroyal miserliness Peter Pindar again is the historian.

> "For, not long since, I heard a forward dame
> Thus, in a tone of impudence, exclaim,
> Good God! how kings and queens a song adore!
> With what delight they order an *encore*!
> When that same song, *encor'd*, for *nothing* flows!
> This Madam Mara to her sorrow knows!
> To Windsor oft, and eke to Kew,
> The r-y-l mandate Mara drew.
> No cheering drop the dame was asked to sip—
> No bread was offer'd to her quivering lip:
> Though faint, she was not suffer'd to sit down—
> Such was the *goodness*—grandeur of the crown.
> Now tell me, will it ever be believ'd,
> How much for song and chaise-hire she receiv'd?
>
> How much pray, think ye? Fifty guineas. 'No.'
> Most surely forty. 'No, no.' Thirty. 'Poh!
> Pray, guess in reason, come again!'—
> Alas! you jeer us!—twenty at the least;
> No man could ever be so great a b—st
> As not to give her twenty for her pain.—
> 'To keep you, then, no longer in suspense,
> For Mara's chaise-hire and unrivall'd note,
> Out of their *wonderful* benevolence,
> Their bounteous M——ies gave—not a groat.'"[217]

The pecuniary treatment accorded to Madame Mara was meted out also to Mrs. Siddons, who, appointed preceptress in English reading to the Princesses, but without salary,[218] was summoned frequently to read or recite at Court, and came out of the palace "as rich as she went in."

> "Such are the stories twain! Why, grant the fact,
> Are *princes*, pray, like *common folks* to act?
> Should Mara call it cruelty, and blame
>   Such r-y-l conduct, I'd cry, Fie upon her!
> To Mrs. Siddons freely say the same,
>   Sufficient for *such people* is the *honour*."[219]

CHAPTER X

THE PRIVATE LIFE OF THE KING AND QUEEN

Shortly after his marriage the King sought a residence where he and his consort should live more free from the ceremony and restraint of court life than was possible at St. James's. Kensington Palace he thought too near the metropolis, and he disliked the "stately, unvaried flatness" of Hampton Court. He did, indeed, invite "Capability" Brown to reorganise the artificial grounds of the latter palace, but that despotic gardener declined, "out of respect for himself and his profession," to do anything more than advise that the trees should be allowed to grow in their natural way.[220] George determined to purchase a mansion and with the Queen inspected Wanstead House, which delighted him. "It is well, Charlotte, you did not stop here on your way to the palace," he said, "for that would have been thought a mean residence after seeing this elegant mansion." However, the many charms of the Essex house were found to be more than counterbalanced by the distance from town and the necessity to pass through the City to reach it; and eventually the King purchased Buckingham House from Sir John Sheffield for £21,000, and subsequently contrived to persuade Parliament to settle this on the Queen in exchange for Somerset House.[221]

From an engraving by W. Knight after a drawing by E. Dayes
BUCKINGHAM HOUSE

Preparations were made at once to equip the building for its royal occupiers, and Walpole in 1762 noted that, "The King and Queen are stripping the other palaces to furnish it. In short, they have already fetched pictures from Hampton Court, which indicates their never living there;

consequently Strawberry Hill will remain in possession of its own tranquillity, and not become a cheese-cake house to the palace. All I ask of princes is not to live within five miles of me." In June, 1762, the sovereigns took up their residence at the "Queen's House," as it was called henceforth, and on the 6th inst. gave a house warming, "for which a most elegant entertainment was planned—a concert, a ball, the gardens to be illuminated, suppers, bands of music, the whole of a magnificent description, under the direction, principally, of Mr. Kuffe, a German, and general invitations to the nobility were to be issued."[222] There, when in London, the King and Queen lived in the strictest privacy, and never went to St. James's but to hold *levées* and drawing-rooms.

The King's love of rural scenery made him spend as much time as possible in the country, and he migrated to Richmond Lodge regularly in the middle of May, returning for the week in which his birthday fell. There he made many improvements, and when the Lodge was found too small to accommodate the increasing family, he discussed plans for a new palace, to be erected close by, with Sir William Chambers.

> "Sir William, cover'd with Chinese renown,
> Whose Houses are no sooner *up* than *down*,
> Don't heed the discontented Nation's cry:
> *Thine* are *religious* Houses, very *humble*
> Upon their *faces* inclin'd to tumble;
> So *meek* they cannot keep their head on *high*."[223]

A model of the proposed design was made and operations begun, only to be suspended, while the ground floor was yet in course of erection, by the refusal of the authorities of the town to sell a small piece of ground essential to the scheme. Thereupon the King determined to remove to Kew, where he had spent large sums on the improvement of the gardens under the direction of Sir William Chambers, who had erected all sorts of buildings, Roman, Greek, Moresque, and Chinese.

> "Be these the rural pastimes that attend
> Great Brunswick's leisure: these shall best unbend
> His royal mind, whene'er from state withdrawn,
> He treads the velvet of his Richmond lawn;
> These shall prolong his Asiatic dream,
> Tho' Europe's balance trembles on its beam."[224]

Subsequently when alterations on an extensive scale were made at Windsor Castle,[225] the people of Richmond, realizing they were in danger of losing their royal residents altogether, offered the land they had before refused; but it was too late, and the enclosure round the abandoned palace was given over to farming.

"Soon after [the marriage] Buckingham House was purchased, and bestowed on her Majesty, St. James's not seeming a prison strict enough," Horace Walpole has written; and in this sentence may be read the key to the first years of Queen Charlotte in England, for during that period she was, indeed, little better than a prisoner, with a gaoler in the form of her duenna (who was also supposed to be a spy of the Princess Dowager) Katherine Dashwood,[226] the "Delia" of James Hammond, who had not been to Court for twenty-five years, when she was a Woman of the Bedchamber to George II's consort. "Except the Ladies of the Bedchamber[227] for half-an-hour a week in a funeral circle, or a ceremonious drawing-room, she [the Queen] never had a soul to speak to but the King," Mrs. Harcourt has recorded in her Diary. "This continued till her first child, the Prince of Wales, was born; then the nurse and governess, Lady Charlotte Finch, coming into the room was a little treat; but they had still for years no other society, till by degrees the Ladies of the Bedchamber came far more frequently, and latterly the society, for various reasons—the children growing up, the journeys, etc.—was much increased. Expecting to be Queen of a gay Court, finding herself confined in a convent, and hardly allowed to think without the leave of her husband, checked her spirits, made her fearful and cautious to an extreme, and when the time came that amusements were allowed, her mind was formed to a different manner of life." Seclusion in a dreary Court at the age of seventeen was not the way to bring out that which is best in a woman's character, and doubtless this had its effect in producing a certain bitterness and hardness that subsequently showed themselves, although some fifty years later the Queen expressed her belief that the course followed had been advisable. "I am most truly sensible of the dear King's great strictness, at my arrival in England, to prevent my making many acquaintances; for he was always used to say that, in this country, it was difficult to know how to draw a line on account of the politics of the country and that there never could be kept up a society without party, which was always dangerous for any woman to take part in, but particularly so for the royal family; and with truth do I assure you that I am not only sensible that he was right, but I feel thankful for it from the bottom of my heart."

Charlotte had hoped to bring with her some of her countrywomen, but she was allowed only to carry with her two dressers, Mrs. Haggerdorn and Mademoiselle Schwellenberg, the latter a shrewd ambitious woman who, not content to play the subordinate part imposed upon her by her office, set herself up as a mentor to the Queen, and no one was to be admitted to her Majesty's presence without having first been introduced to "Mademoiselle."[228] It would doubtless have been a surprise to "Mademoiselle" to learn that she was to achieve immortality, and her astonishment would scarcely have been pleasurable could she have read the passages in Miss Burney's Diary that have procured her that distinction. It would, however, probably have surprised her still more to know that, within a century, for one reader of the annals of the reign of George III there would be scores who eagerly turned over the pages of the journal of the little lady she treated so cavalierly. "I found [silence] equally necessary to keep off the foul fiends of Jealousy and Rivalry of my colleague," wrote Miss Burney,[229] "who, apparently, never wishes to hear my voice but when we are *tête-à-tête* and then never in good humour when it is at rest."

In vain an adulatory biographer of Queen Charlotte[230] has drawn a pleasant portrait of Mademoiselle Schwellenberg, in vain he states she was "a well-educated and highly accomplished woman, extremely courteous in her manner, much respected by all the domestics of the royal household, and devotedly attached to the illustrious family with whom she lived, who, in their turn, entertained for her the sincerest affection. Mademoiselle Schwellenberg had been, however, most cruelly and wantonly held up to public ridicule by a profligate wit, whose delight lay in ribaldry, as a woman of sordid disposition, than which nothing could be more opposite to her real character, for she was ever ready to oblige all who applied to her for assistance; and though, like her royal mistress, she chose to do good by stealth, her charities were very extensive." She lives for all time as Miss Burney's harsh, unsympathetic taskmaster, a stern unbending woman whose overpowering ways eventually caused the King to desire her dismissal, a fate from which she was saved only by the request of the Queen, who was very attached to her,[231] and upon her subscribing to his Majesty's conditions, that she should not resent his commands, nor influence the Queen's mind upon any subject, that she should share the labours with her companion, and infringe upon no regulation unconnected with her immediate appointment.

These instructions the dresser accepted, and, as was only to be expected in a woman of her character, soon ignored, thereby earning the dislike of Mrs. Papendiek, of Frederick Albert, of Fanny Burney, and, of course, of "Peter Pindar," who salvoed a farewell verse when she left the country on a visit to Germany in 1789.

> "With great *respect* I here assure you, Ma'am,
> Your name our common people loudly damn;
> *Genteeler* folk attack with *silent* curses."

Still, the Schwellenberg's devotion to her mistress was undeniable, and her reverence for Majesty so intense that she could not even faintly understand why, when she announced, "Miss Bernar, the Queen will give you a gown," that lady was not overcome with gratitude for the high honour. Perhaps Miss Burney depicted her with a pen dipped too deeply in gall, and certainly she let her anger get the better of her humour, though no excuse for this need be sought, since association with the illiterate old scold day and night for years might well have embittered a more chastened person than the authoress of "Cecilia"; but why she should have borne with the woman's tyranny and capriciousness, and not in return, at least, have chaffed her, as did Colonel Manners and Colonel Grenville, is past understanding.

Why the King and Queen invited Miss Burney to accept the part of dresser on the resignation of Mrs. Haggerdorn in 1786 is a problem only to be solved by the acceptance of Macaulay's belief that it was thought to be an act of kindness. "But their kindness was the kindness of persons raised high above the mass of mankind, accustomed to be addressed with profound deference, accustomed to see all who approached them mortified by their coldness and elated by their smiles. They fancied that to be noticed by them, to serve them, was in itself a kind of happiness; and that Frances Burney ought to be full of gratitude for being permitted to purchase, by the surrender of health, wealth, freedom, domestic affections and literary fame, the privilege of standing behind a royal chair and holding a pair of royal gloves."[232]

It would be as easy as it would be unprofitable to moralize upon the vanity of princes: it is more interesting to inquire why Miss Burney accepted a menial position at Court. She has told us of her consternation when Mr. Smelt brought the unwelcome offer and informed her, "Her Majesty proposed giving me apartments in the palace; making me belong to the table of Mrs. Schwellenberg with whom all her own visitors—bishops, lords, or commons —always dine; keeping me a footman, and settling on me £200 a year." Miss Burney's first impulse was to refuse, but Mr. Smelt's astonishment that she should hesitate, the surprise of Mrs. Delany at her reluctance, and the persuasion of her father undermined her decision, and, swayed perhaps by the fascination that great personages had for her, she accepted the offer, and on July 11 attended the Court in an official capacity. Much pity has been expended upon the famous novelist, and Macaulay has made an attack on Dr. Burney for his share in inducing her to accept; which attack is, perhaps, more brilliant than fair, for Miss Burney was more than thirty years of age, had innumerable unprejudiced friends eager to advise, and was not constrained to accept by poverty, from the grinding pressure of which her pen at this time could save her. Her awe of royalty doubtless had something to do with her going to Court, and it says much for the respect in which the Court was held that she who was well acquainted with many of the most notable persons in England, should lose her self-possession when the King addressed her. "I believe there is no constraint to be put upon real genius; nothing but inclination can set it to work," George said once in her presence, "Miss Burney, however, knows best." Then, hastily returning to her, he cried, "What? what?" "'No, Sir, I—I—believe not certainly,' quoth I, very awkwardly, for I knew not how to put him off as I would another person."[233]

Miss Burney does not seem to have been unhappy at first, although, of course, the uncongenial surroundings and employment soon wearied her. Indeed, she found much amusement in the etiquette of the Court, which alone disqualified her for the post, for the woman who was tickled by the quaintness of her walk backwards in the presence of royalty instead of treating it as a serious matter should have had no place in a royal retinue. Her humour was sufficiently robust in the early days of her employment to draw up for her mother's edification a quaint list of "directions for coughing, sneezing, or moving before the King or Queen."

"In the first place you must not cough. If you find a tickling in your throat, you must arrest it from making any sound; if you find yourself choking with the forbearance, you must choke—but not cough. In the second place, you must not sneeze. If you have a vehement cold, you must take no notice of it; if your nose-membranes feel a great irritation, you must hold your breath; if a sneeze still insists upon making its way you must oppose it by keeping your teeth grinding together; if the violence of the repulse breaks some blood-vessel, you must break the blood-vessel, but not sneeze. In the third place, you must not, upon any account, stir either hand or foot. If, by chance, a black pin runs into your head, you must not take it out. If the pain is very great, you must be sure to bear it without wincing; if it brings the tears into your eyes, you must not wipe them off; if they give you a tingling by running down your cheeks, you must look as if nothing was the matter. If your blood should gush from your head by means of the black pin, you must let it gush; if you are uneasy to think of making such a blurred appearance, you must be uneasy, but you must say nothing about it. If, however, the agony is very great, you may, privately, bite the inside of your cheek, or of your lips, for a little relief; taking care, meanwhile, to do it as cautiously as to make no apparent dent outwardly. And with that precaution, if you even gnaw a piece out, it will not be minded, only be sure either to swallow it, or commit it to a corner of the inside of your mouth till they are gone—for you must not spit."[234]

The irritating complacency of royalty for not blaming her when, for instance, she had been out of doors when wanted within, after a time seemed to Miss Burney but natural; and it is doubtful if she could summon up a smile even for the delightful equerry, Colonel Manners, who once announced, "I think it right to be civil to the King." The iron slowly entered into her soul, and she became as imbued with flunkeyism as the meanest scullion in the royal kitchen. Let those who doubt read her remarks on the trial of Warren Hastings.

The private life of the sovereigns was almost inconceivably dull, and the tedium of the monotonous existence not unnaturally affected them adversely: Charlotte was far from happy, and a marked change came over George. "His [the King's] formerly excellent spirits had evidently forsaken him. Instead of that easy, good-natured, ingratiating familiarity, which had hitherto distinguished him in his intercourse with others, his manner had become distant and cold, and his countenance expressive of melancholy. It was evident to all who approached him that his mind was ill at ease."[235] George endeavoured to find amusement in poking about Windsor, asking questions of all he met in his rambles. "Well, lad, what do you want?" he asked a stable-boy. "What do they pay you?" "I help on the stables," the youngster grumbled, "but I have nothing but victuals and clothes." "Be content," said the monarch, philosophically, "I have no more." Sometimes his inquisitiveness enabled him to redress a grievance, and then he was happy for, according to his lights, he was a just man. Soon after his accession several of the lower servants were dismissed without his knowledge, and one day, entering a cottage near the Castle he saw an old woman engaged in housework, who, assuming that the visitor was one of the royal housemaids, whom she expected, complained, "I have seen better days in the old King's time, but the young King has turned everything topsy-turvy," adding, "I suppose you'll be turned out, too." It is pleasant to learn she was re-instated.

George, indeed, took an active interest in the domestic economy of the palaces, and little that was trivial failed to attract his attention. The system of vails-giving had become a serious tax on the pocket of visitors. It has been told how Sir Timothy Waldo dined with the Duke of Newcastle, and on his departure found the servants lined up awaiting tribute. He paid right and left, and when he came to the cook, put a crown in his hand. "Sir, I don't take *silver*," said the man, returning the coin. "Don't you, indeed?" said the baronet courteously, as he replaced it in his pocket. "Well, I don't give *gold*!" Indeed, the abuse had come to such a pass that many a man could not afford to dine with a friend. Jonas Hanway has amusingly narrated one of his after-dinner experiences, "Sir, your great-coat," said one, upon which he paid a shilling. "Your hat," said another—a shilling—"Your stick"—a shilling

—"Sir, your gloves." "Why, friend, you may keep the gloves," said Hanway, "they are not worth a shilling." After this Hanway wrote his "Eight Letters to the Duke of Newcastle on the custom of Vails-giving in England," which pamphlet was shown by the Duke to the King, who at once summoned the servants of his household, and addressed them: "You come into my service at a stipulated salary; that salary is regularly paid to you; your services are paid by me, nor will I henceforth be subject to the meanness of having my servants paid by the contribution of others. I will not have a single vail taken in my household, and the first who is guilty of the offence shall that instant receive his dismissal. This order applies to you all; therefore as far as my example can extend, the practice of vails-giving shall be abolished."[236] The immediate sequel to this address was an assembly of the royal servants at Drury Lane Theatre on the occasion of the King's visit on March 7, 1761, when the monarch was received with shouts of execration.

A quaint light on the internal economy of the palace is thrown by a letter from the Queen to Lord Harcourt in 1803, that shows that the parody, "The King commands the first Lord-in-waiting to desire the second Lord to intimate to the gentleman Usher to request the page of the Antechamber to entreat the Groom of the Stairs to implore John to ask the Captain of the Buttons to desire the maid of the Still Room to beg the Housekeeper to give out a few more lumps of sugar, as His Majesty has none for his coffee, which is probably getting cold during the negotiations," had a sound basis of fact. "My Lord, I want you to exert your authority in dismissing my footman, Oby, the service as soon as possible, as his unquenchable thirst is now becoming so overpowering, that neither our absence nor our presence can subdue it any more," the Queen wrote. "Some messages of consequence being sent by him to the apothecary's, was found in his pockets when laying dead drunk in the street a few days ago, luckily enough by the Duke of Cumberland, who knowing they were for the family, sent them to Brand; I do not want him to starve, but I will not have him do any more duty. This I hope will be an example to the others; but as I write a Tipling-letter, I think it not amiss to mention that Stephenson has appeared twice a little *Bouzy*, the consequence of which was a fall from his horse yesterday, by which he was very much bruised; and the surgeon who came to bleed him at the Duke of Cambridge's House, who very humanely took him in, declared him to have been at least over dry, if not drunk. A reprimand to him will be necessary; for should it happen again he must go."

From a caricature published in 1786
THE CONSTANT COUPLE

Nothing could exceed the simplicity of the private life of George and Charlotte, the regularity of which was broken only by the frequent confinements of the Queen and the King's illnesses. During the first years of her married life Charlotte every morning read English with Dr. Majendie, a task at which George sometimes assisted. She scarcely knew a word of the language of her adopted country on her arrival, which gave Lady Townshend the opportunity to remark, on hearing that Lady Northumberland had been made a Lady of the Bedchamber, that "it was a very proper appointment, for, as the Queen knew no English, that lady would teach her the vulgar tongue." The first use to which her Majesty put her newly-acquired knowledge was to address poetical effusions to her husband. "I send you verses, *said* to be the Queen's upon the King, it seems impossible that she should write them so soon, but I fancy she wrote in French," Lady Sarah Bunbury wrote to Lady Susan O'Brien in 1764. "Whitehead or somebody translated them; whoever did, they are bad enough."[237] In spite of their lack of merit, one set of verses may perhaps be given as a curiosity:—

> "Genteel is my Damon, engaging his air,
> His face like the morn is both ruddy and fair,
> Soft love sits enthroned in the beam of his eyes,
> He's manly, yet tender, he's fond, and yet wise.
>
> "He's ever good-humour'd, he's generous and gay,
> His presence can always drive sorrow away,
> No vanity sways him, no folly is seen,
> But open his temper, and noble his mien.
>
> "By virtue illumin'd his actions appear,
> His passions are calm and his reason is clear,
> An affable sweetness attends on his speech,

He's willing to learn, though he's able to teach.

"He has promised to love me—his words I'll believe,
For his heart is too honest to let him deceive;
Then blame me, ye fair ones, if justly you can,
Since the picture I've drawn is exactly the man."

After her English lesson, the Queen devoted an hour or two to needlework, and then walked or rode with the King till dinner. In the evening, if there was no company she would sing to her own accompaniment on the spinet, and play cards with her ladies, while the King amused himself at backgammon, a game to which he was devoted. Nothing could be more genteel and more dull. "The recluse life led here at Richmond—which is carried to such an excess of privacy and economy, that the Queen's *friseur* waits on them at dinner, and four pounds only of beef are allowed for their soup—disgusts all sorts of persons," Walpole wrote to Lord Hertford; but while this is probably an exaggeration, the statement is valuable as showing the spirit in which the Court was regarded. Occasionally, of course, there was a little mild gaiety, which usually took the form of an informal dance, for her Majesty was as fond of dancing as of cards, housekeeping and the theatre. "I prefer plays to all other amusements," declared the Queen, who "really looked almost concerned" to learn that Miss Burney had never seen Mrs. Pope, Miss Betterton, or Mr. Murray.[238] When she was at the Queen's House, she went to a theatre once a week, but was careful always to select the piece to be performed, which, as the choice was made presumably after hearing the plot, must have robbed her of much of her enjoyment. This precaution was taken after a visit to see "The Mysterious Husband," when George was so overcome that he turned to his consort, "Charlotte, don't look, it's too much to bear," and commanded it should not be repeated. He, too, was fond of the theatre, liking comedy better than tragedy, and while the Queen's favourites were John Quick and Mrs. Siddons, he preferred Quin and Elliston to all other actors. Both delighted in music, frequently attended the Opera, and gave concerts at St. James's, when the King's band played, when Stanley was organist, Crosdill 'cellist, and Miss Linley sang, until after her marriage, when her place was taken by Madame Bach (*neé* Galli), and Miss Cantilo. As a rule, however, to the great disgust of the majority of the *suite*, only the works of Handel were performed.

From an engraving by W. Woollett
KEW PALACE

"The Kew life, you will perceive, is different from the Windsor. As there are no early prayers, the Queen rises later; and as there is no form or ceremony here of any sort, her dress is plain, and the hour for the second toilette extremely uncertain," Miss Burney wrote. "The royal family are here always in so very retired a way, that they live as the simplest country gentlefolks. The King has not even an equerry with him, nor the Queen any lady to attend her when she goes her airings."[239] At Windsor a certain degree of ceremony was observed, and many old customs preserved. "I find it has always belonged to Mrs. Schwellenberg and Mrs. Haggerdorn to receive at tea whatever company the King and Queen invite to the Lodge," Miss Burney noted, "as it is only a very select few that can eat with their Majesties, and those few are only ladies; no man, of what rank soever, being permitted to sit in the Queen's presence."[240] The King, who was an early riser, worked at affairs of state from six until eight o'clock, when a procession for chapel was formed, headed by the King and Queen, the Princesses following in pairs, and after them the ladies and gentlemen in waiting, who usually attended in full strength, for though it was not obligatory on the members of the suite, their absence was resented by the Queen. "The King rose every morning at six, and had two hours to himself. He thought it effeminate to have a carpet in his bedroom. Shortly before eight, the Queen and the royal family were always ready for him, and they proceeded to the King's chapel in the castle. There were no fires in the passages; the chapel was scarcely alight; Princesses, governesses, equerries grumbled and caught cold; but cold or hot, it was their duty to go; and, wet or dry, light or dark, the stout old George was always in his place to say amen to the chaplain."[241]

After breakfast, the King would either return to his study, or go riding or hunting, two forms of exercise to which he was very partial. Until his illness prevented him, he never missed going with the whole of his family to the races at Ascot Heath, at which place he gave a plate of a hundred guineas, to be run for on the first day by such horses as had hunted regularly with his own hounds the preceding winter.

While the King had the business of state and hunting with which to occupy himself, his consort was less fortunate, for her husband never mentioned public affairs in her presence, and let her understand from the first that this would always be so. Five years after the Royal marriage, Chesterfield remarked, "The King loves her as a woman, but I verily believe has not yet spoken one word to her about business"; and long after Lord Carlisle stated, "The King never placed any confidence whatever in the Queen as to public affairs, nor had she any power either to injure or serve any one. In this respect he treated her with great severity." However, as time passed and children came to her, she found some occupation—as well as much anxiety. "The Queen would have two physicians always on the spot to watch the constitutions of the royal children to eradicate, if possible, or at least to keep under, the dreadful disease, scrofula, inherited from the King," Mrs. Papendiek, assistant-keeper of the Wardrobe and Reader to her Majesty, has told us. "She herself saw them bathed at six every morning, attended the schoolroom of her daughters, was present at their dinner, and directed their attire, whenever these plans did not interfere with public duties, or any plans or wishes of the King, whom she neither contradicted nor kept waiting a moment under any circumstances."[242] As the children grew up, the elder were sometimes allowed to breakfast with their parents, who once a week went with the entire family to Richmond Gardens; but the intercourse was strictly regulated, and the little boys and girls were never allowed to forget that their mother and father were the King and Queen of England. Charlotte tried to find pleasure in her trinkets, and she told Miss Burney how much she liked the jewels at first. "But how soon that was over!" she sighed. "Believe me, Miss Burney, it is the pleasure of a week—a fortnight at most, and to return no more. I thought at first I should always choose to wear them; but the fatigue and trouble of putting them on, and the care they required, and the fear of losing them, believe me, ma'am, in a fortnight's time I longed again for my earlier dress."[243] The poor woman had not even the satisfaction of being popular with her subjects, for the public, which did not love minor German royalties, had not at the first shown any great enthusiasm for the Queen, and such favour as she had found in their eyes very soon declined.

Indeed, it was not long before there was a very marked feeling against her, and this became obvious to all the world when, within a month of her first *accouchement*, she attended a public installation of the Garter.[244] This early reappearance was thought indelicate, and an ill-advised plea put forward by her friends—that her German training must be taken into consideration—only added fuel to the fire, for foreign customs even to-day find little toleration at the hands of this nation whose creed is liberty.

"You seem not to know the character of the Queen: here it is—she is a good woman, a good wife, a tender mother, and an unmeddling queen," Lord Chesterfield wrote to his son in 1765; and a loyal rhymester set forth the same view in a "Birthday Ode," in which he played at satire.

>"The Queen, they say,
>Attends her nurs'ry every day;
>And, like a common mother, shares
>In all her infant's little cares.
>What vulgar unamusing scene,
>For George's wife and Britain's queen!
>'Tis whispered also at the palace,
>(I hope 'tis but the voice of malice)
>That (tell it not in foreign lands)
>She works with her own royal hands;
>And that our sovereign's sometimes seen,
>In vest embroidered by his queen.
>This might a courtly fashion be
>In days of old Andromache;
>But modern ladies, trust my words,
>Seldom sew tunics for their lords.
>What secret next must I unfold?
>She hates, I'm confidently told,
>She hates the manners of the times
>And all our fashionable crimes,
>And fondly wishes to restore
>The golden age and days of yore;
>When silly simple women thought
>A breach of chastity a fault,
>Esteem'd those modest things, divorces,
>The very worst of human curses;
>And deem'd assemblies, cards and dice,
>The springs of every sort of vice.
>Romantic notions! All the fair
>At such absurdities must stare;
>And, spite of all her pains, will still
>Love routs, adultery, and quadrille."

In a Birthday Ode indiscriminate eulogy is expected, and due allowance made for the enthusiasm of the poet, but from a man with the perspicacity of Lord Chesterfield a more critical estimate of the Queen's character might have been anticipated. Leigh Hunt said Charlotte was a "plain, penurious, soft-spoken, decorous, bigoted, shrewd, overweening personage,"[245] and the truth of his description cannot be seriously impugned. That she was not fair to look upon was a misfortune more severe to herself than to others, but her domineering spirit was a sore trial to those who came into contact with her, as readers of Fanny Burney's Diary know. She was very jealous of her influence with the King, clinging to such power as it gave her with remarkable tenacity, and suspicious of those who were dear to him. Thus, when in 1772 the King's sister, the Duchess of Brunswick, visited England at the suggestion of the Princess Dowager, her mother, the Queen did not offer the Duchess the hospitality of a royal palace, but took for her "a miserable little house" in Pall Mall, and contrived that she should not see the King alone. This strange behaviour became generally known and as generally disapproved, with the result that when at this time the King and Queen visited a theatre they were received in chilling silence, but, to mark its feeling, the house vociferously cheered the Duchess of Brunswick on her entry.

Charlotte's faults, however, were probably mostly due to environment. "Bred up in the rigid formality of a petty German court, her manners were cold and punctilious: her understanding was dull, her temper jealous and petulant."[246] She seems to have had affection for the husband to whom, with all her faults, she made a good wife, although she but rarely gave any overt sign of her feeling for him. "The Queen had nobody but myself with her one morning, when the King hastily entered the room with some letters in his hand, and addressing her in German, which he spoke very fast, and with much apparent interest in what he said, he brought the letters up to her and put them into her hand. She received them with much agitation, but evidently of a much pleased sort, and endeavoured to kiss his hand as he held them. He would not let her, but made an effort, with a countenance of the highest satisfaction, to kiss her. I saw instantly in her eyes a forgetfulness at the moment that any one was present, while drawing away her hand, she presented him her cheek. He accepted her kindness with the same frank affection that she offered it; and the next moment they both spoke English, and talked upon common and general subjects. What they said I am far enough from knowing; but the whole was too rapid to give me time to quit the room; and I could not but see with pleasure that the Queen had received some favour with which she was sensibly delighted, and that the King, in her acknowledgments, was happily and amply paid."[247]

Charlotte, however, had no endearing qualities, or, if she had in her youth, they soon became atrophied by the spirit that forced her to put her dignity before all else. A certain Duchess begged the Queen to receive her niece, about whom an unfounded scandal had been circulated. Her request was refused, and, on leaving the royal presence, she made a further appeal, "Oh, Madam! what shall I say to my poor niece?" "Say," replied Charlotte, "say you did not dare make such a request to the Queen." The Duchess at once resigned the post she held at Court, and the Queen made half a score of bitter enemies. She was a hard woman, and had no consideration for her *entourage*. Lady Townshend, who was with child, became greatly fatigued at a royal function at which it was, of course, *de rigeur* to stand, and the Princess of Wales, noticing this, turned to her mother-in-law, and asked, "Will your Majesty command Lady Townshend to sit down?" "She may stand," said Charlotte, petulantly, "she may stand." This was, however, only to be expected in a mother who seldom permitted her offspring to sit in her presence: it is related that when she was playing whist one of her sons fell asleep standing behind her chair. The Duchess of Ancaster suffered by this severe etiquette, but she was a woman of resource, and when in her official capacity she accompanied her royal mistress on a state visit to Oxford, becoming very tired, she drew a small body of troops before her, and, thus sheltered, rested on a convenient bench.

A more favourable picture of Queen Charlotte is drawn by Miss Burney, who thought very highly of her. "For the excellence of her mind I was fully prepared; the testimony of the nation at large could not be unfaithful; but the depth and soundness of her understanding surprised me: good sense I expected; to that alone she could owe the even tenour of her conduct, universally approved, though examined and judged by the watchful eye of multitudes. But I had not imagined that, shut up within the confined limits of a court, she could have acquired any but the most superficial knowledge of the world, and the most partial insight into character. But I find now, I have only done justice to her disposition, not to her parts, which are truly of that superior order that makes sagacity intuitively supply the place of experience. In the course of this month I spent much time alone with her, and never once quitted her presence without fresh admiration of her talents."[248] That Charlotte had common sense combined with strong will may be admitted, nor can it be denied that she could be kind on occasion. She purchased a house in Bedfordshire as a home for poor gentlewomen, and she became the patroness of the Magdalen Hospital; she was gracious to the Harcourts, and was perhaps seen at her best in her intercourse with Mrs. Delany, to whom, after the death of Margaret, Duchess of Portland, the King presented a furnished house at Windsor and an annuity of £300 out of the Privy Purse, the half-yearly payments of which were taken to her by the Queen in a pocket-book, in order that it might not be docked by the tax-collector. The sovereigns met Mrs. Delany for the first time at Bulstrode Park, when George offered a chair to the old lady, who was much confused by his condescension. "Mrs. Delany, sit, down, sit down," said Charlotte, smiling, to set her at her ease, "it is not everybody that has a chair brought her by a King."

Caricature by Wm. Hogarth
JOHN WILKES

CHAPTER XI

"No. XLV"

Lord Bute, to support his policy, had founded two newspapers, "The Auditor," and, under the editorship of Smollett, "The Briton," and these inspired John Wilkes, member of Parliament for Aylesbury, to set up, as a weapon for the Opposition, "The North Briton," the onslaughts in which were so ferocious that "The Auditor" on February 8, 1763, and "The Briton", four days later, died of sheer fright. Wilkes and Charles Churchill,[249] the most valuable contributor to "The North Briton," did indeed fight with the buttons off the foils, and, while other papers still retained the custom of referring to persons by their initials, they disdained this foolish method, and gave their enemies the poor comfort of seeing their names in the full glory of print.

When Bute resigned, No. xliv of "The North Briton" had appeared, and the next issue was in preparation. Wilkes, on hearing this important intelligence, delayed the publication to see if George Grenville,[250] the new Prime Minister, would offer a new policy, or follow in the footsteps of his late leader. Pitt and Lord Temple showed Wilkes an early copy of the King's Speech, and, learning from this that no change would take place, the latter proceeded with the composition of the since historic No. xlv. The King's Speech was read on April 19, 1763, and on April 23 appeared the famous sheet, wherein the terms of the peace, the Cyder tax, and other acts of the Ministry were attacked, and the Address was stigmatised as "the most abandoned instance of ministerial effrontery ever attempted to be imposed upon mankind." In the paper it was stated very clearly that the King's Speech was always regarded, not as the personal address of the sovereign, but as the utterance of ministers. "Every friend of his country," said "The North Briton," "must lament that a prince of so many great and amiable qualities, whom England truly reveres, can be brought to give the sanction of his sacred name to the most odious measures and to the most unjustifiable declarations from a throne ever renowned for truth, honour and unsullied virtue."

This attack on ministers was not more violent than others that had appeared in earlier issues of the same paper, but the adherents of Bute, whom Wilkes had taken an active part in ousting from the Ministry, now saw an opportunity to avenge their fallen leader. The severe criticism of his speech made the King furious, and on the principle of *"L'état, c'est moi,"* he disregarded the distinction that Wilkes had so carefully drawn between the utterances of the monarch and the utterances of ministers in the monarch's name, and encouraged, if, indeed, he did not instigate, a prosecution. The Secretary of State, Lord Halifax, issued a general warrant, that is, a warrant which specified neither the name nor names nor described the person nor persons of the offender or offenders, but only gave instructions "to make a strict and diligent search for the authors, printers and publishers of a seditious and treasonable paper entitled 'The North Briton,' No. xlv, Saturday, April 23, 1763, printed for G. Kearsley, in Ludgate Street, London, and them, or any of them, having found, to apprehend and seize, together with their papers, etc."

The printer and publisher were at once arrested, and, when brought before Halifax and Egremont, gave the names of the authors as John Wilkes and Charles Churchill. The warrant was shown to Wilkes at his house in Great George Street on the night of April 29, but he declined then to comply with it, stating his objection to a general warrant as such, pointing out that his name was not mentioned, that he was a Member of Parliament, and concluded by threatening the first who should offer violence to him in his own house at that hour of the night; but when the officers returned in the morning he offered no further opposition. Just after he was arrested and before he had been removed from his house, Churchill walked into the room, where were Wilkes and his captors. Wilkes knew the messengers wanted also to arrest Churchill, and observing they did not know the poet by sight, before the latter could speak, with great presence of mind, said, "Good morning, Mr. Thomson. How is Mrs. Thomson to-day? *Does she dine in the country?*" Churchhill took the hint, said Mrs. Thomson was waiting for him, left the room, and fled from the metropolis.

Wilkes's papers were seized, and he was taken before the Secretaries of State, and by them, after he had asserted his privileges as a Member of Parliament and had refused to answer any questions, was committed a prisoner to the Tower. Such were the preliminaries of the great battle that made Wilkes a great and popular figure in the struggle for the liberty of the subject and the liberty of the press in England.

Wilkes's friends moved at once for a writ of *habeas corpus*, and after some delay, on May 6, the prisoner was produced before Chief-Justice Pratt[251] in the Court of King's Bench, when counsel applied for his discharge on the ground that the commitment was not valid. The Judge gave his decision in favour of Wilkes, declaring that general warrants were illegal, and that, anyhow, the charge against the accused was not sufficient to destroy his privileges as a Member of Parliament.

Wilkes was no sooner at liberty than he showed he was not a man who could be maltreated with impunity. He republished the numbers of "The North Briton" in a volume with notes, reasserting that the King's Speech could only be regarded as a ministerial pronouncement. He addressed to Lord Halifax and Lord Egremont an open letter, of which many thousand copies were distributed throughout the country, complaining that his home had been robbed, and that he was informed that "the stolen goods are in possession of one or both of your Lordships." His papers were not returned, and he brought an action against Robert Wood, the Under-Secretary of State, against whom he received a verdict giving £1,000 damages, and another action against Lord Halifax for unlawful seizure, from whom also, after many years' delay, he recovered heavy damages. In the meantime Lord Egremont had written to Lord Temple that the King desired the latter, as Lord-Lieutenant of the county, to inform Wilkes that he was dismissed from the Colonelcy of the Buckinghamshire Militia, which task Temple duly discharged, saying, "I cannot, at the same time, help expressing the concern I feel in the loss of an officer, by his deportment in command, endeared to the whole corps." As a punishment for this expression of sympathy, the King removed Lord Temple from the Lord-Lieutenancy, and with his own hand struck his name out of the Council books.

> "To honour virtue in the Lord of Stowe,
> The pow'r of courtiers can no further go;
> Forbid him Court, from Council blot his name,
> E'en these distinctions cannot rase his fame.
>
> Friend to the liberties of England's state,
> 'Tis not to Courts he looks to make him great;
> He to his much lov'd country trusts his cause,
> And dares assert the honour of her laws."[252]

The ministers in this struggle had found a powerful ally in Hogarth, who, though he had been friendly with Wilkes and Churchill, had been high in Bute's favour, even before the accession of George III, and now saw an opportunity to repay his patron. The quarrel between the painter and the agitator had begun with Hogarth's political cartoon, "The Times," in which Wilkes was ignominiously portrayed; and Wilkes, who let no man attack him with impunity, had replied in "The North Briton" with a violent onslaught upon the caricaturist. When Wilkes appeared in the Court of King's Bench, Hogarth, it is said, from behind a screen made a sketch for a caricature of the accused, in which the latter's squint was most malignantly exaggerated. Wilkes took this in good part, and, indeed, in later days said jocularly that he found himself every day growing more and more like the unflattering portrait; but Churchill, who was devoted to his friend, replied in "An Epistle to William Hogarth," in which—after the model furnished by Pope in his immortal reprimand to Addison—while praising Hogarth's genius, he poured vitriolic scorn upon his vanity and other weaknesses, concluding with a tremendous indictment of the painter's supposed dotage.

> "Sure, 'tis a curse which angry fates impose,
> To mortify man's arrogance, that those

Who're fashioned of some better sort of clay,
Much sooner than the common herd decay.
What bitter pangs must humbl'd Genius feel
In their last hours to view a Swift and Steele!
How must ill-boding horrors fill her breast,
When she beholds men mark'd above the rest
For qualities most dear, plunged from that height,
And sunk, deep sunk, in second-childhood's night!
Are men, indeed, such things? and are the best
More subject to this evil than the rest?
To drivel out whole years of idiot breath,
And set the monuments of living death?
Oh, galling circumstance to human pride!
Abasing thought, but not to be denied!
With curious art the brain, too finely wrought,
Preys on herself, and is destroyed by thought.
Constant attention wears the active mind,
Blots out her powers, and leaves a blank behind.
But let not youth, to insolence allied,
In heat of blood, in full career of pride,
Possess'd of genius, with unhallow'd rage
Mock the infirmities of reverend age;
The greatest genius to this fate may bow;
Reynolds, in time, may be like Hogarth now."

Hogarth replied to the "Epistle" by a savage caricature of Churchill, entitled, "The Bruiser, C. Churchill (once the Reverend!) in the character of a Russian Hercules, regaling himself after having killed the monster *Caricatura*, that so sorely-galled his *virtuous* friend, the Heaven-born Wilkes." The poet is portrayed as a bear, with torn clerical bands and ruffles, seated upon Massinger's "A New Way to Pay Old Debts," and "A List of the Subscribers to 'The North Briton,' etc., one arm holding a quart pot, and the other round a massive club, on which the knots are inscribed "Lye 1," "Lye 3," "Lye 5," "Lye 8," "Fallacy," etc.

A caricature of C. Churchill by Wm. Hogarth
THE BRUISER

Ministers, having been defeated on a point of law, were now determined to ruin Wilkes,[253] and proceeded, so far as lay in their power, to damn his reputation for all time, although, as will be seen, the method adopted did not have the desired effect.

That Wilkes was a man of high moral character, as some few of his eulogists have endeavoured to sustain, is a theory incapable of acceptance, though perhaps his lack of principle in early days has been more severely castigated than it deserved, considering that morality is, after all, comparative, and that a dragon of virtue in the days that were earlier would now be looked upon as a monster of iniquity. The son of a rich merchant, Wilkes was educated in England and at Leyden, and on his return to England at the age of two-and-twenty, had been persuaded by his father to espouse a wealthy woman ten years his senior. Not unnaturally the marriage was unhappy, and, indeed, Wilkes never even professed to regard it except as a convenience, but notwithstanding this circumstance his behaviour to his wife leaves the deepest stain on his character. He squandered her money in debauchery, and, after they had separated, endeavoured to deprive her of an annuity of £200 a year, all she had kept of her estates. He was initiated by Sir Francis Dashwood into the brotherhood of Medmenham Abbey, where he fraternised with Lord Sandwich,[254] Thomas Potter,[255] and other men of fashion, and with them proceeded to outrage all canons of decency.[256] In connexion with the brotherhood Potter and Wilkes in collaboration composed an obscene parody of Pope's "Essay on Man" called "An Essay on Woman," which, in imitation of the original poem, was furnished with notes under the name of Bishop Warburton; and to the burlesque was attached a blasphemous paraphrase of *Veni Creator*.

Without setting up any defence of these compositions, it may in extenuation be said that the circulation was limited to twelve or thirteen copies, which were distributed among members of the club, that it was printed at Wilkes's house, and that the latter took the greatest care to prevent the workmen from carrying away any sheets. Disgraceful as the amusement was, at least it could be pleaded it had no evil effect upon the circle of vicious men who inspired it; but it gave the Government a handle against their uncompromising foe of which they were not slow to take advantage.

In spite of all precautions, one of the printers had stolen some sheets of the "Essay on Woman" and this fact, which came to the knowledge of John Kidgell, then chaplain to the Earl of March, was by him imparted to a minister, who incited the clergyman to publish a pamphlet giving an account of Potter and Wilkes's *jeu d'esprit*. This in itself was an unworthy proceeding, but a greater folly threw this into the shade, for, when it was decided to bring to the notice of Parliament the stolen copy of the "Essay," the person chosen to raise the matter in the House of Lords was Lord Sandwich, than whom, Mr. Justin McCarthy has rightly said, "no meaner, more malignant, or more repulsive figure darkens the record of the last century."[257] This was a bad blunder, for Sandwich, as a member of the Franciscan brotherhood at Medmenham, had received a copy of the production, had read it with amusement, and had expressed his approval; and, even apart from this, was notorious for profligacy even among his immoral associates—rumour has it he was expelled for blasphemy from the Beefsteak Society, and Horace Walpole has stated that "very lately, at a club with Mr. Wilkes, held at the top of the play-house in Drury Lane, Lord Sandwich talked so profanely that he drove two harlequins out of the company."[258]

> "Hear him but talk, and you would swear
> Obscenity itself were there,
> And that Profaneness had made choice,
> By way of trump, to use his voice;
> That, in all mean and low things great,
> He had been bred at Billingsgate;
> And that, ascending to the earth

> Before the season of his birth,
> Blasphemy, making way and room,
> Had mark'd him in his mother's womb."[259]

At the moment, to make bad worse, it was known that Sandwich had some personal animus against Wilkes, arising out of a quarrel at an orgy at which Sandwich when very drunk had invoked the devil, and Wilkes had thereupon let loose a monkey and nearly scared his fellow reprobate out of his wits. What the public thought of the part Sandwich took in this affair was not long afterwards made manifest at a performance at Covent Garden Theatre of "The Beggar's Opera," when, in the third act, Macheath exclaims, "That Jemmy Twitcher should peach me I own surprised me. 'Tis a proof that the world is all alike, and that even our gang can no more trust each other than other people," there were cries from all parts of the house of "Jemmy Twitcher! Jemmy Twitcher!" and for the rest of his life by that sobriquet was Sandwich known, even, as Horace Walpole says, to the disuse of his own name.

> "Extremes in nature prove the same,
> The profligate is dead to shame,
> No conscious pangs ensue;
> Satire can't wound the virtuous heart,
> Nor *Savile* fell her venom'd dart,
> No more, my lord, than you.
>
> "To peach the accomplice of one's crimes,
> A gracious pardon gains sometimes,
> When treachery recommends;
> For you, my lord, is clearly seen,
> For close the sacred tie between
> King's evidence and friends."[260]

Parliament met on November 15, 1763; and Lord Sandwich, before the Address was taken into consideration, placed on the table the "Essay on Woman," and denounced it as a "most blasphemous, obscene, and abominable libel," in a speech which drew from Lord le Despencer the remark that never before had he heard the devil preach. Bishop Warburton's language on this occasion was, perhaps, such as no divine has ever before or since employed in public—"the blackest fiends in Hell would not keep company with Wilkes," he declared, and then apologised to Satan for comparing them. This intemperance of attack coupled with the underhand methods employed by the Ministry, brought forth a remonstrance from Pitt; while later Churchill avenged Wilkes by some lines of terrible ferocity on the Bishop:

> "He drank with drunkards, lived with sinners,
> Herded with infidels for dinners;
> With such an emphasis and grace
> Blasphemed, that Potter kept not pace:
>
> He, in the highest reign of noon,
> Bawled bawdy songs to a Psalm tune;

> Lived with men infamous and vile,
> Truck'd his salvation for a smile;
> To catch their humour caught their plan,
> And laughed at God to laugh with man;
> Praised them, when living, in each breath,
> And damn'd their memories after death."[261]

The House of Lords voted the "Essay" a breach of privilege, a "scandalous, obscene and impious libel," and presented an address to the King demanding the prosecution of the author for blasphemy; while at the same time the House of Commons declared No. xlv of "The North Briton" to be a "false, scandalous, and seditious libel," and ordered the paper to be burnt by the common hangman. In the debate in the lower house, Samuel Martin, an ex-Secretary of the Treasury, who had been denounced in "The North Briton" as a "low fellow and a dirty tool of power," took the opportunity to denounce Wilkes as a cowardly, scandalous, and malignant scoundrel, and immediately afterwards challenged him to a duel, in which the latter was severely wounded. Wilkes, although the challenged person, had generously allowed his assailant the choice of weapons, and Martin selected pistols. Subsequently, however, it became known that, since the insult appeared in "The North Briton" eight months earlier, he had regularly practised shooting at a target, whereupon Churchill took the not unnatural view that Martin was, to all intents and purposes, a would-be assassin.

> "But should some villain, in support
> And zeal for a despairing Court,
> Placing in craft his confidence,
> And making honour a pretence
> To do a deed of deepest shame,
> Whilst filthy lucre is his aim;
> Should such a wretch, with sword or knife,
> Contrive to practise 'gainst the life
> Of one who, honour'd through the land,
> For Freedom made a glorious stand;
> Whose chief, perhaps his only crime,
> Is (if plain Truth at such a Time
> May dare her sentiments to tell)
> That he his country loves too well;
> May he—but words are all too weak
> The feelings of my heart to speak—
> May he—oh, for a noble curse,
> Which might his very marrow pierce!—
> The general contempt engage,
> And be the Martin of his age!"[262]

Though Wilkes was confined to his house by his wound, ministers, in spite of his petition that no further steps should be taken before his recovery, pressed forward their measures against him. During the Christmas recess Wilkes became convalescent and went to France, from whence, when Parliament reassembled, he sent a medical certificate stating he was unable to travel without endangering his health; but his enemies declared, and perhaps some of his friends secretly believed, that this was a subterfuge, and that in reality the reason for his continued absence was because he dared not face the trials for libel and blasphemy. On January 19, 1764, Wilkes was expelled from the House of Commons for having written a scandalous and seditious libel; and on February 21 the Court of King's Bench found him guilty of having reprinted "No. XLV" and of printing the "Essay on Woman," and, as he did not appear to receive sentence, outlawed him for contumacy.

Ministers now congratulated themselves upon having got rid of their dangerous opponent, but, as a matter of fact, they had only driven him away, which was a very different thing, for in his absence he, standing as the persecuted champion of liberty, was a very potent factor in affairs. Lord Temple paid the greater part of Wilkes's law expenses, and, subsequently, the Rockingham Whigs made the outlaw an allowance of £1,000 a year. Wilkes's popularity was, indeed, immense. When on December 3, "No. XLV" was to be burnt at the Royal Exchange, a great mob collected, and showed so threatening a spirit that Harley, one of the sheriffs, went to consult the Lord Mayor as to what steps should be taken to avert danger, and the hangman followed in his wake. The partly-burnt copy of "The North Briton" was rescued by the crowd, carried off in triumph, and displayed in the evening at Temple Bar, where a bonfire was made into the midst of which, amidst great cheering, a huge jack-boot was thrown. Chief Justice Pratt was rewarded for his impartial judgment with the freedom of the cities of London and Dublin; and all adherents of Wilkes became popular personages. Astute tradesmen disposed easily of inferior goods by marking them "45," and the turmoil created by this affair penetrated even the recesses of the Court, with the result that some years later the young Prince of Wales, when he had been punished, avenged himself by crying in his father's presence "Wilkes and No. XLV for ever!"

Kearsley, the publisher of "The North Briton" was discharged by the Court on his own recognizances; but in 1765 Williams, who had re-issued "No. XLV" was fined £100, ordered to stand in the pillory in Old Palace Yard for an hour on March 1, and to give security in the sum of £1,000 for his good behaviour for seven years. This was an opportunity that gave Wilkes's supporters a chance to display their feelings. Williams was taken in a triumphant procession in a hackney-coach numbered forty-five and brought back in the same way; while he stood in the pillory a collection was made, and £200 subscribed for him; and close by were erected four ladders, with cords running from each other, on which were displayed a jack-boot, an axe, and a Scotch bonnet, to testify to the prevalent belief that the moving spirit of the prosecution was Lord Bute.

"THE PILLORY TRIUMPHANT, or, No. 45 FOR EVER.

"Ye sons of Wilkes and Liberty,
  Who hate despotic sway,
The glorious forty-five now crowns
  This remarkable day.
    And to New Palace Yard let us go, let us go.

"An injured martyr to her cause
  Undaunted meets his doom:
Ah! who like me don't wish to see
  Some great ones in his room?
    Then to New Palace Yard let us go, let us go.

"Behold the laurel, fresh and green,
  Attract all loyal eyes;
The haughty thistle droops his head,
  Is blasted, stinks, and dies.
    Then to New Palace Yard let us go, let us go.

"High mounted on the gibbet view
  The *Boot* and *Bonnet's* fate;
But where's the *Petticoat*, my lads?
  The *Boot* should have its mate.
    Then to New Palace Yard let us go, let us go.

[Pg 254]

"In vain the galling *Scottish yoke*
  Shall strive to make us bend;
Our monarch is a Briton born,
  And will our rights defend.
    Then to New Palace Yard let us go, let us go.

"For ages still might England stand,
  In spite of Stuart arts,
Would Heaven send us men to rule
  With better heads and hearts.
    Then to New Palace Yard let us go, let us go."

For a while, engaged in an amorous adventure, Wilkes remained at Paris, but in 1767 he issued a pamphlet explaining his position, and just before the general election of March, 1768, he reappeared in London[263] and offered himself as a candidate for the parliamentary representation of the City, thus presenting the very strange spectacle, as Lecky puts it, "of a penniless adventurer of notoriously infamous character, and lying at this very time under a sentence of outlawry, and under a condemnation for blasphemy and libel, standing against a popular alderman in the metropolis of England."[264] In spite of his late appearance upon the scene, Wilkes polled 1,200 votes; and, thus encouraged, and supported by Lord Temple, who furnished the necessary freehold qualification, the Duke of Portland, and Horne Tooke, he stood for the county of Middlesex, and was elected by 1,290 votes against 827 of the Tory George Cooke and 807 of the Whig, Sir William Procter.

As Wilkes had received no reply to his petition for a pardon addressed to the King, he, according to the undertaking he had given, surrendered himself on the first day of term, April 20, before Lord Mansfield in the Court of King's Bench. The proceedings dragged on until June 8, when, his outlawry having been annulled, he was sentenced for republication of "No. XLV" to a fine of £500 and ten months' imprisonment, and for the printing of the "Essay on Woman" to another fine of £500 and a further twelve months' imprisonment. The populace, delighted to have their hero again among them, escorted him to prison, illuminated their houses, and broke the windows of those who took no part in the rejoicings, with the result that there ensued a riot in which six people met their death.

The election of Wilkes to the House of Commons perplexed ministers, who at first sought refuge in inaction, but eventually, after much provocation from the new member[265] moved to expel him from Parliament and carried their resolution by 219 to 137 votes. This, however, led only to further trouble, for when a new writ for Middlesex was issued, Wilkes was re-elected on February 16. Again, on the following day, he was expelled, and a resolution passed that he was incapable of sitting in the existing Parliament. This was clearly illegal, and the people avenged this attempted infringement of their rights by returning Wilkes for the third time on March 16. On the 17th he was once more expelled; and, when returned once more, a few days later, the House of Commons by 197 to 143 votes declared the defeated candidate, Colonel Luttrell,[266] duly elected.

The popularity of Wilkes was gall and wormwood to the King, whose authority and wishes were openly set at defiance, and who was openly threatened by the mob. It was known he had taken an active part in the prosecution of the popular demagogue, and this was deeply resented. "If you do not keep the laws, the laws will not keep you," so ran the lettering of a placard thrown at this time into the royal carriage. "Kings have lost their heads for their disobedience to the laws." George III's courage was undeniable, and no threat could make him connive at any action likely to lessen the royal prerogative. "My spirits, I thank heaven, want no rousing," he wrote to Lord Chatham in May, 1767. "My love to my country, as well as what I owe to my own character and to my family, prompt me not to yield to faction. Though none of my ministers stand by me, I cannot truckle."[267] Lord North, too, was well acquainted with the royal firmness and intrepidity: "The King," he said, "would live on bread and water to preserve the constitution of his country. He would sacrifice his life to maintain it inviolate."

The courage George III displayed in politics was not lacking in moments of personal danger. Though, unlike George I and George II, he could not prove his valour on the field of battle, the several attacks upon his life gave him sufficient opportunity to show his fearlessness. It was, indeed, at these times he appeared at his best, not only in dignity, but in kind-heartedness and in tender consideration for his consort. The first murderous attack upon him was made August 2, 1786, as he alighted from his coach at the garden entrance of St. James's Palace. A woman, Margaret Nicholson, held out to him a paper, which, assuming it to be a petition, he took from her; but as he did so she struck at him with a knife, and the attempt to kill him only failed from the knife being so thin about the middle of the blade that, instead of entering the body, it bent with the pressure of his waistcoat.[268] The would-be assassin was at once seized, and seeing she was roughly handled, "The poor creature is mad," cried the King; "do not hurt her. She has not hurt me." He held the *levée*, and then drove hastily to Windsor to let the Queen know he was unhurt. "I am sure you must be sensible how thankful I am to Providence for the late wonderful escape of his Majesty from the stroke of an assassin," Mrs. Delany wrote to Miss Hamilton. "The King would not suffer any one to inform the Queen of that event till he could show himself in person to her. He returned to Windsor as soon as the Council was over. When his Majesty entered the Queen's dressing-room he found her with the two eldest Princesses; and entering in an animated manner, he said, "Here I am, safe and well!" The Queen suspected from this saying that some accident had happened, on which he informed her of the whole affair. The Queen stood struck and motionless for some time, till the Princesses burst into tears, on which she immediately found relief."[269]

From an old print

THE KING'S LIFE ATTEMPTED

Thirteen years later, on October 29, 1795, on his way to open Parliament, he was surrounded by a violent mob, who threw stones into the carriage, and demanded peace and the dismissal of Pitt. Lord Onslow, who was with the King, has left an account of the distressing incident. "Before I sleep let me bless God for the miraculous escape which my King, my country, and myself, have had this day. Soon after two o'clock, his Majesty, attended by the Earl of Westmoreland and myself, set out for St. James's in his state coach, to open the session of Parliament. The multitude of people in the park was prodigious. A sullen silence, I observed to myself, prevailed through the whole, very few individuals excepted. No hats, or at least very few, pulled off; little or no huzzaing, and frequently a cry of 'give us bread': 'no war': and once or twice, 'no King'! with hissing and groaning. My grandson Cranley, who was on the King's guard, had told me, just before we set out from St. James's that the park was full of people who seemed discontented and tumultuous, and that he apprehended insult would be offered to the King. Nothing material, however, happened, till we got down to the narrowest part of the street called St. Margaret's, between the two palace yards, when, the moment we had passed the Office of Ordnance, and were just opposite the parlour window of the house adjoining it, a small ball, either of lead or marble, passed through the window glass on the King's right hand and perforating it, leaving a small hole, the bigness of the top of my little finger (which I instantly put through to mark the size), and passed through the coach out of the other door, the glass of which was down. We all instantly exclaimed, 'This is a shot!' The King showed, and I am persuaded, felt no alarm; much less did he fear, to which indeed he is insensible. We proceeded to the House of Lords, when, on getting out of the coach, I first, and the King immediately after, said to the Lord Chancellor, who was at the bottom of the stairs to receive the King, 'My Lord, we have been shot at.' The King ascended the stairs, robed, and then perfectly free from the smallest agitation, read his speech with peculiar correctness, and even less hesitation than usual. At his unrobing afterwards, when the event got more known (I having told it to the Duke of York's ear as I passed under the throne, and to the others who stood near us), it was, as might be supposed, the only topic of conversation, in which the King joined with much less agitation than anybody else. And afterwards, in getting into the coach, the first words he said were, 'Well, my Lords, one person is *proposing* this, and another is *supposing* that, forgetting that there is One above us all who *disposes* of everything, and on whom alone we depend.' The magnanimity, piety, and good sense of this, struck me most forcibly, and I shall never forget the words.

"On our return home to St. James's, the mob was increased in Parliament Street and Whitehall, and when we came into the park, it was still greater. It was said that not less than 100,000 people were there, all of the worst and lowest sort. The scene opened, and the insulting abuse offered to his Majesty was what I can never think of but with horror, or ever forget what I felt, when they proceeded to throw stones into the coach, several of which hit the King, which he bore with signal patience, but not without sensible marks of indignation and resentment at the indignities offered to his person and office. The glasses were all broken to pieces, and in this situation we were during our passage through the park. The King took one of the stones out of the cuff of his coat, where it had lodged, and gave it to me, saying, 'I make you a present of this, as a mark of the civilities we have met with on our journey to-day.'"[270]

In connexion with this episode an accusation of ingratitude was brought against the King. "Now the tradition is," wrote Lady Jerningham, "that at a certain critical moment, when the guards had actually been pushed back or disorganized for a while by a rush of the rabble, a gentleman sprang forward in front of the carriage door, drew on the assailants, threatening to kill forthwith any one who approached nearer, and thus kept the mob at bay sufficiently long to allow the guards to rally round the coach, and prevent further assault. The King inquired about 'the name of his rescuer,' and was informed that it was Mr. Bedingfeld."[271] According to Lady Jerningham, "no further notice was taken," but this was not so, although there was some delay, owing to Mr. Bedingfeld's sense of humour offending a minister. The King instructed Dundas to give his preserver an appointment of some profit, and Dundas asked Bedingfeld what could be done for him, to which question came the witty but unfortunate reply: "The best thing, sir, you can do for me is to *make me a Scotchman*." Dundas angrily dismissed the humorist, but George, after making frequent inquiries as to what had been done, and each time receiving the reply that no suitable position was vacant, at last said very tartly: "Then, sir, you must *make* a situation for him," and a new office with a salary of £650 a year was created for Mr. Bedingfeld.

Twice more and on the same day, May 31, 1800, was the King's life in danger. In the morning he was present at a review of the Grenadier Guards in Hyde Park, and during one of the volleys of, presumedly, blank cartridge, a bullet struck Mr. Ongley, a clerk in the Admiralty, who was standing only a few paces from his Majesty. It was never discovered, however, whether this accident was deliberate or unintentional. George visited Drury Lane Theatre the same evening, and the moment he appeared in his box, a man in the pit near the orchestra discharged a pistol at him. "It's only a squib, a squib; they are firing squibs," he reassured the Queen as she entered the box; and, when the man was removed, "We will not stir," he added, "but stay the entertainment out." "No man ever showed so much courage as our good

King's disregard of his person, and confidence in the overshadowing Providence on the pistol being fired," Lady Jerningham wrote. "He went back one step and whispered to Lord Salisbury: it is now known that it was to endeavour to stop the Queen, for that it was likely another shot would be fired, he himself remaining at his post. The Queen, however, arrived a moment after, and he then said they had fired a squib."[272] When Sheridan said to the King that after the shot he should have left the box lest the man fired again, "I should have despised myself for ever, had I but stirred a single inch. A man on such an occasion should need no prompting but immediately see what is his duty," the latter rejoined; and indeed he had his nerves so well under control that "he took his accustomed doze of three or four minutes between the conclusion of the play and the commencement of the farce, precisely as he would have done on any other night."[273] "I am going to bed with a confidence that I shall sleep soundly," he said later in the evening, "and my prayer is that the poor unhappy person, who aimed at my life, may rest as quietly as I shall." It was *à propos* of this attempt that Sheridan at once composed an additional verse for the Royal Anthem, which was sung at the conclusion of the performance.

> "From every latent foe,
> From the assassin's blow,
> God save the King!
> O'er him Thine arm extend;
> For Britain's sake defend
> Our father, Prince, and friend;
> God save the King!"

In spite of these attacks, which had no political significance, for the perpetrators, Margaret Nicholson and James Hatfield, were mad, the King would have no guards except on state occasions, and when remonstrated with by a member of his Court, "I very well know that any man who chooses to sacrifice his own life may, whenever he pleases take away mine, riding out, as I do continually, with a single equerry or footman," he said calmly. "I only hope that whoever may attempt it will not do it in a barbarous or brutal manner."[274]

A king who could face death without a tremor was not to be frightened by any demagogue.

"Though entirely confiding in your attachment to my person, as well as in your hatred of every lawless proceeding," he wrote to Lord North on April 25, "yet I think it highly proper to apprise you that the exclusion of Mr. Wilkes appears to be very essential, and must be effected."[275]

The King's anger greatly handicapped ministers. "The ministers are embarrassed to the last degree how to act with regard to Wilkes," the Bishop of Carlisle wrote to Grenville. "It seems they are afraid to press the King for his pardon as that is a subject his Majesty will not easily hear the least mention of; and they are apprehensive, if he has it not, that the mob of London will rise in his favour."[276] When the City of London presented an address, complaining of the arbitrary conduct of the House of Commons, the King burst out laughing and turned his back on the Lord Mayor. A second deputation was treated in much the same way, when the Lord Mayor, William Beckford, replied to the King's abrupt reply with an impromptu speech, that was subsequently inscribed on a monument erected in his honour in the Guildhall. "Permit me, Sire, further to observe that whosoever has already dared, or shall hereafter endeavour, by false insinuations, and suggestions, to alienate your Majesty's affections from your loyal subjects in general, and from the City of London in particular, is an enemy to your Majesty's person and family, a violator of the public peace, and a betrayer of our happy constitution as it was established at the glorious and necessary revolution."

While Wilkes was in prison his admirers paid his debts, it is said, to the amount of £17,000, and on his release on April 17, 1770, he was greeted with as much enthusiasm as a king on his coronation. "It seemed," as Heron remarked, "as if the population of London and Middlesex were the *plebs* of ancient Rome, and Wilkes a tribune." The Common Council of the City elected him, in quick succession, Alderman and Sheriff, and, after the Court of Aldermen had twice selected another candidate, he became Lord Mayor in 1774, the year that witnessed his return for the fifth time as Member of Parliament for Middlesex, "Thus," said Walpole, summing up the career of this indomitable man, "after so much persecution by the Court, after so many attempts upon his life, after a long imprisonment in gaol, after all his own crimes and indiscretions, did this extraordinary man, of more extraordinary fortune, attain the highest office in so grave and important a city as the capital of England, always reviving the more opposed and oppressed, and unable to shock Fortune, and make her laugh at *him* who laughed at everybody and everything."

In the end, however, Wilkes made his peace with the King, was received at Court, and became somewhat of a courtier, declaring that himself had never been a Wilkite. The strange spectacle of the monarch and the demagogue engaged in amicable conversation delighted Byron, who could not miss so excellent an opportunity for humour.

> "Since old scores are past
> Must I turn evidence? In faith not I.
> Besides, I beat him hollow at the last,
>   With all his Lords and Commons: in the sky.
> I don't like ripping up old stories, since
> His conduct was but natural in a prince.

Foolish, no doubt, and wicked, to oppress

    A poor unlucky devil without a shilling;
But then I blame the man himself much less
    Than Bute and Grafton, and shall be unwilling
To see him punished here for their excess,
    Since they were both damn'd long ago, and still in
Their place below: for me, I have forgiven,
And vote his *habeas corpus* into Heaven."[277]

THE KING & JOHN WILKES.

O rare Forty five!
O dear Prerogative!

The Wolf shall dwell with the Lamb, & the Leopard shall lie down with the Kid; & the Calf & the young Lion. & the Fatling together: & a <u>little</u> Child [A] shall lead them.

[A] Vide, Pitt.

Isaiah. Chap. xi.V.v

THE RECONCILIATION

CHAPTER XII

THE KING UNDER GRENVILLE

The King accepted Lord Bute's resignation without regret, and indeed made so little secret of his pleasure that, according to Lord Hardwicke, he appeared "like a person just emancipated," for, in spite of his personal feeling for his old friend, he thought that as a minister Bute had shown a deplorable lack of political firmness. Bute's day as a public official had passed for ever, and not the most subtle intrigue of the Princess Dowager could induce her son even to discuss the question of the ex-minister's return to power, although for some time to come he was, as we shall see, a power in the closet, and, indeed, with one exception, it is said, chose the members of the Cabinet of his successor.

"I do not believe that the King ever wished to reinstate the Earl of Bute," Nicholl wrote subsequently. "He saw the earl's want of courage; probably he saw his incapacity, and his unfitness to serve his views: but it is possible that the Princess Dowager of Wales might still retain a wish that the Earl of Bute should be replaced in the office of Prime Minister."

When Grenville first came into office the King's regard for the new Prime Minister was so great as to lead him to declare that "he never could have anybody else at the head of his Treasury who would fill that office so much to his satisfaction."[278] Grenville was in many ways acceptable to George. "His official connexion with Bute, his separation from the great Whig families, his unblemished private character, his eminent business faculties, his industry, his methodical habits, his economy, his freedom alike from the fire and the vagaries of genius, his dogged obstinacy, his contempt for popularity, were all points of affinity."[279]

Grenville came into office to protect the King from the Whigs, and, indeed, was appointed on condition that none of the Newcastle and Pitt ministry were to be included in the new administration, although he was assured favour might be shown to those Whigs who would support the Government. It soon became obvious, however that the King had only exchanged one set of rulers for another. He had thought to have found in Grenville a pliant tool: he discovered too late he had placed himself in the hands of a harsh task-master. The qualities that George and Grenville had in common, while uniting them at first, very shortly came between them. Both were fond of power, both yielded only under compulsion, both were untactful and ignorant of the soft answer that turneth away wrath. The Minister made no attempt to ingratiate himself with the King, and his attitude reduced the latter to a state of fury, not the less violent because at the moment he was impotent.[280] Grenville's overbearing manner drew from George the complaint, "When I have anything proposed to me, it is no longer as counsel, but what I am to obey;" while his tedious prolixity was a further trial. "When he has wearied me for two hours," George complained to Lord Bute, "he looks at his watch to see if he may not tire me for an hour more."[281]

From a painting by Wm. Hoare
THE RIGHT HON. GEORGE GRENVILLE

Indeed, Grenville possessed most of the qualities unsuitable for the First Minister of the Crown. He had the advantage of courage and ability, but was a near-sighted politician, an ungracious colleague, and a bad speaker; and, while he had a keen eye for the main chance so far as himself was concerned, was unwisely penurious for the revenue. He made an implacable enemy of the King, when the latter took in a portion of the Green Park to form a new garden for Buckingham House, by declining to purchase for the Crown at the cost of £20,000 a plot of ground, now known as Grosvenor Place, on which houses were to be built that would overlook the royal family in their private walks.[282]

The King, finding his head in a noose, made strenuous efforts to extricate himself. In April, 1763, Grenville had become Prime Minister: in July George sought the advice of Bute how to rid himself of his *bête noir*, and then and there made overtures to Hardwicke and Newcastle, who, however, declined to accept office without their party. After the death of Lord Egremont early in August, Bute suggested a coalition, and sent Sir Harry Erskine to Alderman Beckford to arrange a meeting between himself and Pitt. Pitt received Bute at his house in Jermyn Street, and, presumably, the conversation was not unsatisfactory, for on the 23rd inst. the King sent for him and asked him to state his views. Pitt inveighed against the ignominious peace, and complained of the compulsory retirement of the Whigs, who, if he accepted office, must be restored to power. As a matter of fact, the Whigs were not inspired with any kindly feeling towards George, who, in pursuance of his policy that he must be ruler of the realm, had inflicted on their leaders several petty slights. When the Duke of Devonshire,[283] "the Prince of the Whigs," who had declined to take part in the discussion about the peace, had called at St. James's in October, 1762, George, to mark his displeasure, had sent a message by a page, "Tell the Duke I will not see him." The Duke at once resigned his post as Lord Chamberlain, and his brother, Lord George Cavendish, retiring from the Household, was received with marked discourtesy, as was also Lord Rockingham,[284] who, remonstrating with the King for his incivility, surrendered his office in the Bedchamber. Not content with these signs of his annoyance, George struck out the Duke's name from the list of Privy Councillors,[285] deprived the Duke of Newcastle, the Duke of Grafton,[286] and Lord Rockingham, of the Lord-Lieutenancies of their respective counties, and dismissed the great majority of Whigs who held minor offices not usually vacated at a change of ministry. Even military men who voted against the Government on the question of general warrants were deprived of their commands, which was going even farther than Rigby approved[287], though the King declared, "Firmness and resolution must be shown and no one saved who dared to fly off."[288]

The King was in a quandary. He was anxious to dismiss Grenville, but at least as desirous to avoid a Whig administration which, after the indignities inflicted on the leaders, would scarcely be friendly: still, in his conversation with Pitt, he went so far as to offer to accept Lord Temple at the Treasury, and, declaring "his honour must be consulted," gave Pitt an appointment for an interview two days later. Pitt thought the matter was settled, and communicated with his friends, who were consequently elated. "Atlas has left the globe to turn on its own axis," said Charles Townshend, referring to Grenville's absence from town during these negotiations. "Surely he should be prompt when public credit labours, and he either mistakes the subject or slights the difficulty. This man has crept into a situation he cannot fill. He has assumed a personage his limbs cannot carry. He has jumped into a wheel he cannot turn. The summer dream is passing away. Cold winter is coming on; and I will add to you that the storm must be stood, for there will be no shelter from coalition, nor any escape by compromise. There has been too much insolence in the use of power; too much injustice to others; too much calumny at every turn." The hopes of the Opposition were, however, dashed to the ground, for when it came to the point, George could not bring himself to accept the Whigs *en bloc*, and, on the 25th inst., after Pitt had reiterated his terms, dismissed him, saying, "Well, Mr. Pitt, I see this will not do. My honour is concerned, and I must support it."

There was now no other course open to the King than to ask Grenville to remain in office, to which request the minister assented, but only after delivering to the King a lecture on the duty of a sovereign to be loyal to his recognized advisers, and extracting from him a promise that Lord Bute should never again interfere in affairs of state. Yet, in spite of this undertaking, it became known to the Prime Minister that, a few days later, Bute attempted to reopen negotiations with Pitt. Thereupon, Grenville, justly indignant, reproached the King, who promised that nothing of the sort should happen again, to which the minister replied drily that he hoped not, and forthwith set about insuring himself against further interference by insisting on Bute's retirement from London, and refusing to allow the office of Keeper of the Privy Purse, which Bute vacated, to be given to one of the latter's friends. "Good God! Mr. Grenville," exclaimed the King, "am I to be suspected after all I have done?"

The King, who made a "skilful but most dishonourable use of the incautious frankness of Pitt in the closet,"[289] contrived to sow dissension among the Whig leaders, and by these unworthy devices contrived to excite the anger of the Duke of Bedford, whom, through the instrumentality of Lord Sandwich, he, in September, 1763, persuaded to accept the post of President of the Council. About the same time Lord Shelburne,[290] who had been intriguing against Grenville, resigned the Presidency of the Board of Trade, partly because he thought he was not sufficiently considered in the ministerial councils, and partly because he very heartily hated his colleagues. It is said further that he doubted the legality of the proceedings against Wilkes, though his enemies scoffed at the idea of his having any motive so disinterested. He resigned office on September 3, and afterwards voted with Fitzmaurice, Calcraft and Barré against the Government, for which offence the King removed his name from the list of *aides-de-camp*, and deprived Barré of his posts of Adjutant-General of the Forces and Governor of Stirling Castle.

In spite of the unpopularity of the Duke of Bedford, which arose out of his share in the negotiations for the peace, the changes strengthened the administration, and for a while George, somewhat mollified by Grenville's attitude towards Wilkes, and being in full agreement with the ministerial policy towards America, lived in comparative harmony with his advisers. This agreeable state of affairs was soon, however, to be rudely disturbed.

The King was taken ill on January 12, 1765, and on the following day Sir William Duncan informed the Prime Minister that his Majesty had a violent cold, had passed a restless night, complained of stitches in his breast, and was bled fourteen ounces. On the 15th inst. Grenville went to the King, and "found him perfectly cheerful and good-humoured, and full of conversation," after which date no one saw the King, not even his brothers, and it was not until March that Lord Bute, who in the interval had pressed to see him, was admitted for the first time to his presence.[291] The King was suffering from mental derangement, but such were the precautions taken, that this was not known beyond the Palace:[292] the illness was declared to be the outcome of cold and fever, and this announcement, when the confinement threatened to be lengthy, was supplemented by the statement that a humour, which should have appeared in his face, had by unskilful treatment been allowed to settle on his chest. The public anxiety was not assuaged by these bulletins, and, convinced that something was being withheld, jumped to the conclusion that the King was in a consumption. So well was the secret kept that Nicholls wrote in 1819, "I know it has been said that his illness was a mental derangement, but I do not believe it";[293] and Wraxall about the same time remarked, "George the Third was attacked by a disorder that confined him for several weeks; relative to the nature and seal of which malady, though many conjectures and assertions have been hazarded, in conversation, and even in print, no satisfactory information has ever been given to the world."[294] Even George Grenville was in ignorance of the nature of the disorder. At the beginning of March there was a marked improvement in George's condition, and when Grenville saw him on the 18th inst. he noted "the King's countenance and manner a good deal estranged, but he was civil and talked upon several different subjects;" and a week later, when he was again admitted to the royal presence, he "found his Majesty well to all appearance."[295] On April 5, completely recovered, the King held a *levée*.

It has been hinted that the first traces of mental derangement had shown themselves in June, 1762, when Lord Hardwicke informed Lord Royston, "I fear his Majesty was very ill, for physicians do not deal so roughly with such patients without necessity." "It is amazing and very lucky that his Majesty's illness gave no more alarm, considering that the Queen is with child, and the law of England has made no provision for government when no king or a minor king exists," Henry Fox noted. "He goes out now, but he coughs still;

and, which no subject of his would be refused or refuse himself, he cannot or will not go to lie in the country air; though if there was ever anything malignant in that of London since I was born, it is at this time."[296] Walpole, too, heard of the trouble, though he, like the rest, was in ignorance of the nature of the malady, but he was perturbed by the lack of any measure for carrying on the government in the event of the King's illness or demise. "Have you not felt a pang in your royal capacity?" he wrote on June 20, 1762. "Seriously, it has been dreadful, but the danger is over. The King had one of the last of those strange and universally epidemic colds, which, however, have seldom been fatal. He had a violent cough and oppression on his breast which he concealed, just as I had; but my life was of no consequence, and having no physicians-in-ordinary, I was cured in four nights by James's powders, without bleeding. The King was blooded seven times and had three blisters. Thank God, he is safe, and we have escaped a confusion beyond what was ever known, but on the accession of the Queen of Scots."

Though nothing was done in 1762, on his recovery in March, 1765, the King realized it was imperative to make provision for a regency in case of his incapacity or death, and suggested he should be empowered to name a person in his will, while, to "prevent faction," keeping the nomination secret.[297] This, of course, could not be permitted; but it was decided that a Bill should be introduced by ministers, and a reference to it was made in the King's Speech on April 24: "My late indisposition, though not attended with danger, has led me to consider the situation in which my kingdoms and my family might be left, if it should please God to put a period to my life while my successor is of tender years."

A Bill was brought in, limiting the King's choice of a regent to the Queen or any other person of the royal family, and a question arose whether the Princess Dowager was a member of the royal family. When this was decided in the affirmative, the Duke of Bedford, who was anxious to prevent Bute from the exercise of even indirect control of affairs, persuaded Lord Halifax and Lord Sandwich to tell the King that, if the Princess Dowager's name were included, the House of Commons would reject it. The King, desirous to avoid the chance of such an insult to his mother, yielded to the ministers' representations, and the Princess Dowager was pointedly excluded. That is one version of the story, but Lord Hardwicke gives another. After stating that the Duke of Cumberland was much hurt that the princes of the blood were not to be named in the Council of Regency, he relates, "While the Regency Bill was in the House of Lords, the clause naming the King's brothers was concerted, with the Duke of Cumberland, unknown to the ministry till the King sent it to them. They, to return the compliment, framed the clause for omitting the Princess Dowager, and procured the King's consent to it. This raised a storm in the interior of the palaces; and the result of it, after many intrigues and jarrings, was the overthrow of that administration."[298] Walpole, on the other hand, thought that ministers conceived that the omission of the Princess would be universally approved. "They flattered themselves with acquiring such popularity by that act, that the King would not dare to remove them."[299] Whether the motive was desire of popularity or revenge, the move was a great mistake. George soon learnt that the danger was purely fictitious, and thereupon, with tears in his eyes, he begged Grenville to reinsert the name of the Princess Dowager; but the Prime Minister, though he had been no party to the manœuvre practised by the secretaries of state, declined to abandon his colleagues, and would undertake to give way only if the House of Commons pressed the point. In the Lords the Duke of Richmond had moved that the regency should consist of the Queen, the Princess Dowager and all the descendants of the late King usually in England, and Lord Halifax accepted the Duke's words with the single omission of the Princess Dowager, to which amendment the House agreed. "The astonishment of the world is not to be described," Walpole wrote to Lord Hertford, "Lord Bute's friends are thunderstruck; the Duke of Bedford almost danced about the House for joy." The surprise of the friends of the Princess Dowager, however, soon gave way to indignation, and, during the second reading of the Bill in the House of Commons, Morton, the member for Abingdon and Chief Justice of Chester, well known to be in the excluded lady's confidence, moved, with the King's approval and at the suggestion of Lord Northington, the insertion of her Royal Highness's name, which, as the Government could not vote in full strength against their master's mother, was carried by 167 to 17 in the Commons and without a dissentient in the Lords. [300]

George believed he had been deliberately deceived by Lord Halifax and Lord Sandwich, and furious at the unnecessary insult to his mother in which he had been led to participate, on May 6, through the medium of Lord Northumberland, asked his uncle, the Duke of Cumberland, to undertake the charge of negotiations that might lead to the return to office of Pitt, Lord Temple, and the great Whig families.[301] This seems a strange proceeding to Englishmen to-day, when a minister who has a majority in the House of Commons is practically immovable; but then the King, who could appoint a minister, could on his own initiative dismiss him, the only difficulty being to secure a successor. The power of appointment and dismissal of a government is, of course, still the prerogative of the sovereign, but it is impossible to say what would happen were any attempt made to exercise the nominal privilege. In this particular case there was some reason for the King's action, for the weakness of the existing administration was notorious. "The Regency Bill has shown such a want of concert and want of capacity in the ministers, such an inattention to the honour of the Crown, if not such a design against it; such imposition and surprise upon the King; and such a misrepresentation of the disposition of the parliament to the sovereign that there is no doubt that there is a fixed resolution to get rid of them all (except perhaps of Grenville), but principally the Duke of Bedford," Burke wrote to Henry Flood. "Nothing but an intractable temper in your friend Pitt can prevent a most admirable and lasting system from being put together, and this crisis will show whether pride or patriotism be predominant in his character; for you may be assured he has it in his power to come into service of his country, upon any plan of politics he may choose to dictate, with great and honourable terms to himself and to every friend he has in the world, and with such a stretch of power as will be equal to everything but absolute despotism over the King and kingdom. A few days will show whether he will take this part, or that of continuing on his back at Hayes, talking fustian, excluded from all ministerial, and incapable of all parliamentary, service. For his gout is worse than ever; but his pride may disable him more than his gout."[302]

Burke had gauged the situation to a nicety. Pitt was the only man who could form a strong and lasting administration, and he showed no alacrity to accept the invitation. In the meantime the King's impatience got the better of him, and when on May 18 Grenville waited on him with the draft of the speech with which his Majesty should close the session, the following conversation took place. "There is no hurry," said the King; "I will have Parliament adjourned, not prorogued." "Has your Majesty any thought of making a change in your Administration?" "Certainly," was the reply. "I cannot bear it as it is." "I hope your Majesty will not order me to cut my own throat?" "Then," said the King, "who must adjourn the Parliament?" "Whoever your Majesty shall appoint my successor," replied the minister; and thereupon intimated that in a few days he and his colleagues would tender their resignations. Again the King had dismissed his ministers without having made arrangements for their successors, and again he was faced with the problem how the government was to be carried on in the interval. "This is neither administration nor government," Walpole wrote to Lord Hertford. "The King is out of town; and this is the crisis in which Mr. Pitt, who could stop every evil, chooses to be more unreasonable than ever."

Pitt, who at this time was living in retirement, had in October, 1764, told the Duke of Newcastle he intended to remain unconnected, but, when now approached, he was not unwilling to accept office, if he might restore officers and others who had been removed for opposition to the Court, if he might declare general warrants illegal and amend the notoriously unpopular Cyder Act, if "ample justice and favour" might be shown to Chief-Justice Pratt (who was in disgrace at Court owing to his judgment in the Wilkes case), and if he was at liberty to enter into an alliance with continental powers against the Bourbons.[303] When it appeared likely that these points would be conceded, Lord Temple would not undertake to join a ministry formed to displace his brother,[304] and, as Pitt would not take office without his brother-in-law, to whom he was deeply attached and greatly indebted for much kindness, the negotiations fell through. Unable to find relief for his nephew in this quarter, the Duke of Cumberland made ineffectual overtures first to Lord Lyttelton[305] and, subsequently, to Charles Townshend, after which he felt bound to advise George to recall Grenville.

The King had an interview with Grenville on May 22, and on the following day the ex-ministers met to decide the terms on which they would return to office. "The King is reduced to the mortification—and it is extreme—of taking his old ministers again," Walpole wrote to Lord Hertford. "They are insolent enough, you may believe. Grenville has treated his master in the most impertinent manner, and they are now actually discussing the terms that they mean to impose on their captive."

Ministers demanded that Lord Bute should not interfere directly or indirectly in the affairs of Government and that his brother, Stuart Mackenzie, [306] should be dismissed from the office of Keeper of the Privy Seal of Scotland; that Lord Holland should be deprived of the Pay-mastership of the Forces, which should in future be held by a member of the House of Commons; that the Marquis of Granby should be head of the army, and that the government of Ireland should be left to the discretionary arrangement of the ministry.[307] The King was furious and, but that he was impotent at the moment, would have unhesitatingly refused even to discuss most of these conditions. The only concession he could obtain was from Lord Granby, who waived his claim to be Captain-General during the life of the Duke of Cumberland. Lord Holland had to go, although the King, who was bound to him by ties of gratitude, would gladly have retained him; and ministers were united as to the dismissal of Mackenzie, and would not even allow the King's plea that he had promised Mackenzie the post for life and that he would disgrace himself by breaking his word, to weigh with them in the least. Even George's tears made no impression on Grenville and his colleagues, though his embarrassment affected Mackenzie himself, who in spite of the fact that he had accepted his present position at the King's request in exchange for another and more lucrative office, which was desired for some one else, surrendered the Privy Seal without demur. "His Majesty sent for me to his closet, where I was a considerable time with him, and if it were possible to love my excellent Prince now better than I did before, I should certainly do it, for I have every reason that can induce a generous or a grateful mind to feel his goodness to me," Mackenzie wrote to Sir Andrew Mitchell. "But such was his Majesty's situation at that time, that had he absolutely rejected my dismissal, he would have put me in the most disagreeable position in the world, and, what was of much higher consequence, he would have greatly distressed his affairs."[308]

Grenville without delay appointed Lord Frederick Campbell Privy Seal, Charles Townshend Paymaster, and Lord Weymouth Lord Lieutenant of Ireland. The humiliation of the King could go no deeper, nor was it appreciably mitigated by his refusal to appoint Lord Waldegrave Master of the Horse to the Queen—her Majesty said no minister should interfere in *her* family—and appointed the Duke of Ancaster; by his bestowal of the command of the first regiment that fell vacant on Lord Albemarle's brother, General Keppel; or by the paying of marked attention to the young Duke of Devonshire.[309] Indeed, these signs of defiance were met by the minister with a remonstrance which took an hour to read, regretting that the King's authority and the King's favour did not go together. "If I had not broken out into the most profuse sweat," said the unhappy monarch, "I should have been suffocated with indignation."[310]

"Upon the strength of Mr. Pitt's refusing the King, the Duke of Bedford, Lord Sandwich, and G. Grenville have insulted the King," Lady Sarah Bunbury wrote to Lady Susan O'Brien, on June 22, 1765. "They told him that as he could get no others he must take them, but they would not come in positively without such and such conditions, one of which was turning out Mr. Mackenzie. The poor man has been obliged to swallow the pill, but his anger is turned to sulkiness, and he never says a word more than is necessary to them, and sees Mr. Pitt and the Duke of Cumberland constantly. I think he ought to have been violent and steady at first, but since he once submitted he had better not behave like a child now. Everybody must allow they are great *fools* for behaving so to him; they will repent it."[311] Lady Sarah's view of the situation was right: the ministers had over-reached themselves, and their attempts to reduce the King to a cypher forced him in self-defence to make a further desperate effort to shake off the galling yoke. The time was propitious: the members of the administration were quarrelling among themselves, and their handling of the "Weaver's Riots" gave proof to the country of their incapacity. Yet Grenville apparently never dreamt that his position was assailable. "The excessive self-conceit of Grenville, that could make his writers call him—if he did not write it himself—the greatest minister this country ever saw, as well as his pride and obstinacy, established him," Lord Holland wrote to George Selwyn on August 4. "It did not hurt him that he had a better opinion of himself than he, or perhaps anybody else ever deserved. On the contrary, it helped him. But when the fool said upon that—'the King cannot do without me,' *hoc nocuit*."

The Duke of Cumberland again undertook the charge of the negotiations, and renewed the overtures to Pitt, who this time came to town, and on June 19 was with the King for two hours, a fact that became known to Lord Sandwich. Grenville, the Duke of Bedford, and Lord Halifax were in the country, and Sandwich, alarmed, pressed Grenville to return to town, which, however, the Prime Minister declined to do. "When I took leave of the King I asked his permission to stay in the country till Thursday next, which he granted to me," he wrote. "My return to town before that time, uncalled for, will have the appearance of a desire to embarrass the arrangement which he is now endeavouring to form, and which I need not tell you will come on, or go off, just the same whether I am there or not; as the King would not in the present situation communicate it to me, and, without that, I certainly should not trouble him on the subject."[312]

On the 22nd inst. Pitt was closeted with the King for three hours, and it seemed as if he would take office, as, indeed, he might have done if left to himself. "Now Mr. Pitt and the King, and the Duke and the King have long conferences every day. What they will do no mortal can tell, but it's *supposed* that George Grenville and Mr. Pitt are very well together, as Lord Temple has made it up with him, and therefore that they won't come in to turn out Mr. Grenville and the present administration."[313] Lord Temple, however, who cherished a desire that "the brothers"[314] should form a government of their own, would not accept office, whereupon Pitt informed the King he was not prepared to form a cabinet. This he did reluctantly, and it is said, remarked sadly to Lord Temple:

> "*Exstinxti me, teque, soror, populumque patremque Sidonios, urbemque tuam.*"[315]

"All is now over as to me, and by a fatality I did not expect," Pitt wrote to Lady Stanhope on July 20. "I mean Lord Temple's refusing to take his share with me in the undertaking. We set out to-morrow morning for my seat at Burton Pynsent in Somersetshire, where I propose, if I find the place tolerable, to pass not a little of the rest of my days."[316] In the meantime, however, and as a last resource, the Duke of Cumberland turned to the Rockingham Whigs, and, after much negotiation, on July 10, Lord Rockingham accepted office.

END OF VOL. I